YOU CAN PICK ME UP
AT PEGGY'S COVE

YOU CAN PICK ME UP
AT PEGGY'S COVE

Brian Doyle

GROUNDWOOD BOOKS
HOUSE OF ANANSI PRESS
TORONTO   BERKELEY

Copyright © 1979 by Brian Doyle
New paperback edition 2006
First published in the USA in 2006

Groundwood Books / House of Anansi Press
110 Spadina Avenue, Suite 801, Toronto, ON M5V 2K4
Distributed in the USA by Publishers Group West
1700 Fourth Street, Berkeley, CA 94710

ONTARIO ARTS COUNCIL
CONSEIL DES ARTS DE L'ONTARIO

We acknowledge for their financial support of our publishing
program the Canada Council for the Arts, the Government of Canada through
the Book Publishing Industry Development Program (BPIDP)
and the Ontario Arts Council.

Library and Archives Canada Cataloguing in Publication
Doyle, Brian
You can pick me up at Peggy's Cove / by Brian Doyle.
First published, 1979.
ISBN-13: 978-0-88899-709-8   ISBN-10: 0-88899-709-4
I. Title.
PS8557.O87Y6 2006   jC813'.54   C2005-907063-3

Cover photograph by Tim Fuller
Design by Michael Solomon
Printed and bound in Canada

Thanks,
Patsy Aldana and Marilyn Kennedy,
for all your help

Sea Savour

Half a hundred Seagulls
   Standing on a glinting Mound,
   Like snow-white points in a granite Crown;
      Facing each, — and every way,
      Cleave to Glacial moss and clay
On a sea-washed Boulder.

So still, the bright-hued grasses
   With mist rising out at sea…
      Cool, pale, is the sun today, —

A buoy whistles sonorously!
Ominous uncertainty…

from *A Trunk Under My Bed* by Charlotte Duff

1

Listen.

People say that when a dad runs away from home it's harder on the daughter than on the son. That's not true. I'm a boy and I think it's harder on the son.

You see, my dad ran away and so Mum sent my sister, Megan, to Vancouver, where she had to stay with my uncle for the summer and sent me to Peggy's Cove in Nova Scotia to stay with Aunt Fay.

Mum said she was going to spend the summer alone at home in Ottawa concentrating on how to get Dad to come back. He was acting funny because of the C.O.L. The C.O.L. is when someone gets to be about forty-five years old and starts acting a little different because they start thinking about dying or getting old and all that. C.O.L stands for Change Of Life. My grandmother made up the initials so that when she and Mum were talking about it and us kids were

11

around, we wouldn't know what it was. Some people think it's some kind of a secret or something. So I asked Mum right away and she told me the whole thing. Mum doesn't believe in hiding stuff from kids. Especially by using initials.

Anyway, the C.O.L. makes them do funny things. I guess the right word is unpredictable. Like when Dad threw our radio through the kitchen window because of something some announcer said about the metric system. The radio and all the broken glass landed on the hood of our neighbor's car. The radio was talking very loudly by now and Dad stuck his head through the broken window and our neighbor was standing there staring at the radio and Dad asked him very politely if he could turn down the volume a bit. You should have seen the look on that guy's face! Actually, you should have seen the look on Dad's face too!

There was also the time when something happened to our car on the Queensway and Dad just got out and left it there and didn't tell anybody. Then when Mum asked him where the car was he said he lost it.

Once, he made a big speech about how stupid our cat is. It was raining and the cat wanted in the back door. He let the cat in and right away it went to the front door and wanted out. Our cat always does that.

It figures that it might not be raining out the front door and it could go out there and lie in the sun.

"This is the stupidest cat on the planet Earth! It's lived in this house for almost nine years and still thinks things are different out the front than out the back. And look at the stupid smile on its face. This cat is a moron!"

Then he picked up the cat and put his face right up to it. "It rains on both sides of the house! Both sides. Front and back. Get it? It rains out here and out there. It's called OUTSIDE. That's what it's called!"

The cat put its ears away back and just smiled at him. And Dad smiled back as if he felt they really had understood each other.

A few days later my dad ran away from home.

And so I was off to Peggy's Cove for the summer.

Mum took me out to the Ottawa airport and gave me a few last instructions. She told me about clothes and helping Aunt Fay and not worrying. She said she'd let me know where Dad was the minute she found out.

I noticed she gave me a longer hug than usual and I felt like I might cry but I knew I'd better not.

On the way down the ramp to the plane I looked back once, to wave to her, but she was already heading out. She was walking quite fast, almost marching, like she does when she's determined to get something done.

On the plane the man in the seat beside me kept letting his knee rest over on my leg. I hate that. It makes me worried. I don't know if he knew he was doing it or not but that didn't matter. I still didn't like it. So I put both my knees against the wall, turned my back on him and stuck my face right in the little window.

All I could see were clouds, for the whole time we were in the air. Clouds and the engine attached to the wing bouncing up and down as though the wing was going to break off any minute.

I started thinking about dad to get my mind off the plane crash that was coming up.

I was thinking of how dad always used to try to get me to read before I went to sleep at night. He always read a book at night before he went to sleep. He wanted me to do the same. He was always throwing different books on my bed and getting me to try them.

"Just read the first page," he'd say, "you might find it interesting."

But I was more interested in electronics then. I was making my own stereo with disco lights attached and a switch panel to work the lights to the music. I had an old dictaphone pedal that my grandmother gave me and I was hooking it up to my panel. That's what I used to work on at night in bed instead of reading.

Dad would peek in my room and see me sitting there in bed with the blanket covered with wire and tape and parts for my panel and jacks and stuff for my amp that I found in the garbage behind the TV store down the street from us.

"How's the reading going?" he'd say, with his head stuck in the door. Then he'd see the stuff all over my blanket and get a kind of disgusted look on his face.

Then one night when we were both in our rooms in bed with our lights on and Mum was downstairs he called to me, "Why don't you bring your book in here and we'll read together? I'll read my book and you read yours."

I knew he'd be insulted if I didn't go so I got all the wire I was stripping off the blanket and grabbed the nearest book I could find.

It was a *Consumers Distributors* catalog.

I got into his bed on Mum's side and switched on her light and propped the book up just like he had his propped up.

Then he glanced over and saw what I was reading.

"That's not a *book*!" he said, and started sighing and getting that look on his face.

15

I knew he was going to do that so I had something all planned.

I switched out the light, got up and went to the door, quite dramatic, and I did a door speech like they do on TV. Did you ever notice in movies or on TV, people always go to a door, open it, turn around and make a speech, then go out? I call that a door speech.

I grabbed the door handle, turned around and said, "Don't you know that I'm not like you? I'm different than you are. I'm not the same. Do I have to do everything that *you* do?"

Then I went out and slammed the door.

Later on Dad told me that he thought it was a very good speech and then he told me about a door speech he once made which was a failure.

One day, at his job, Dad told his boss off. Then he tried to slam the door but it was hooked up to one of those things that wouldn't let it slam, so the door floated closed as polite as anything and ruined his whole speech. Poor old Dad! He always made me laugh when he told me these stories.

I was thinking other things about Dad and watching the engine on the wing of the plane bouncing up and down.

I was thinking that if the engine fell off the plane we'd crash and everybody'd be killed except me and I'd end up in some hospital in Halifax and I'd wake up and see Dad standing there beside my bed.

I guess I was sighing and stuff because the man beside me asked me if I was scared and I started thinking that his knee would come at me again.

I just ignored him and kept on thinking about Dad and wondering why he'd taken off like he had.

Soon the light went on telling us to fasten our seat belts and all of a sudden we came out of the clouds and I could see Halifax and the ocean down below.

And I guess I don't have to tell you this but we didn't crash.

2

Before I knew it I was in the car with Aunt Fay heading for Peggy's Cove.

My Aunt Fay has a beautiful face. Her eyes are very wide apart and her forehead covers a large space which Dad says is a sign of intelligence.

When she laughs she puts her head back and opens her mouth and her body shakes but she doesn't make any laughing noises. At first she just shakes. Then just about the time she's finished laughing she lets out one sound. Like a dog making one little bark at night if he's tied up in the yard and he's lonesome and it's raining a bit.

Anyway, Aunt Fay was telling me about having my own room upstairs at her place in the house behind the store and how I'd have time to explore everything in Peggy's Cove because I'd have almost two months there and Peggy's Cove wasn't very big. She was telling me that even though Peggy's Cove was small there were enough interesting things there to keep me busy.

"Are there any kids my age there?"

"No. There are only about thirty houses in the whole town and the kids are all grown up and gone away. Some stayed to become fishermen but not very many. There'll be thousands of kids there but they'll just be passing through. Tourists' kids. You won't get to know any of them for any longer than three hours."

We were driving along the coast, right close to the ocean. I couldn't keep my eyes off it. So much water. Some blue, some green, some black. The only other time I'd seen an ocean was when Dad took us out West. I don't remember the Pacific Ocean very well. I guess I was too young or too tired then or something to appreciate it.

"Could we stop and go close to the ocean?"

"Sure."

We pulled up a little side road and parked and got out and walked across a beach and I climbed up on some rocks and stood with my hands on my hips watching the white foam rip up through the cracks in the rocks and the green water sucking back.

I was scaring myself thinking some crazy things, mostly about Dad. It must have been the ocean noise and salty smell that made me start up. Maybe he was drowned or something. I was imagining I could see him floating up on one of the waves. His jacket was all puffed up and his hair was floating like seaweed. Why would he just go away like that? It was making me dizzy and a little sick and I heard Aunt Fay telling me that we had to go.

Back in the car we were talking about C.O.L. When I mentioned it Aunt Fay banged the steering wheel a few times and threw her head back and barked a bit.

"Are they still using those initials? I remember when I was a child I'd hear them say it. We had a neighbor who used to run out in the street at night in her underwear in the snow and sing opera. When she'd do that, everybody would start shaking their heads and whispering 'C.O.L.' For years I thought it meant Crazy Old Lady."

I was feeling a little better and getting excited about the trip. The traffic was getting pretty heavy and Aunt Fay was filling me in about Peggy's Cove. Thousands of people visit there every day but there is no place for a visitor to stay overnight, no hotels or rooms for rent or campsites. And it's the most looked-at place in all Canada probably but that's all most people get to do there, just look.

"But you're lucky. You'll get to do more than look.

You'll be living here. You can get to know the boats. You can watch the fish being brought in and cleaned, you can explore up and down the coast, you can go up to the restaurant and the lighthouse, you can work in my gift shop and help me…"

"Has Dad ever been here?"

"Yes. Once."

"What did he do when he was here?"

"Tease the tourists, mostly."

I could tell she wanted to get my mind off Dad because she started telling me more about Peggy's Cove. She told me how everybody knows about it all over Canada because the picture of it is always on TV and in magazines and on post cards and so when people go sightseeing along the Atlantic they all go to Peggy's Cove and stay a few hours and then take off somewhere else.

And she told me that it was the perfect fishing village because of the boats and the wharfs and the rocks and the lighthouse and the fishermen and how because it was perfect everybody wanted to take a picture of it.

Then she told me that every perfect place has a perfect spot in it to take the perfect picture.

"My shop is right in front of the perfect place where everybody likes to stand with their cameras to take the perfect picture of the perfect fishing village," she told me.

21

She said that you never very often see the real people who live there because they're always in their houses or gone to Halifax or out in their boats and so all you ever see most of the time are the people who only come there for a few hours to buy stuff and take that perfect picture.

The traffic was getting thicker and we were just crawling along. Aunt Fay was still talking about how fish and tourists are the only two ways to make money in Peggy's Cove and how her gift shop and the restaurant were the two main meeting places and how I even might get to go fishing.

We were right behind a huge Winnebago, when the whole line of traffic stopped altogether. I couldn't sit still any longer. I got out of the car and took a walk up the line of traffic. Everybody was leaning out and blowing horns and shouting. The line was full of campers and trailers and vans and tons of stuff. I stopped beside one Winnebago. The windows were filled with the faces of grannies and little kids. The kids were crying and the grannies were staring straight ahead. On the roof they had bicycles and tricycles and canoes and a boat. On the back they had their spare tire with a motorcycle tied to it. Behind they were towing a Volkswagen. On top of the Volkswagen there was other stuff too, tents and barbeques and coolers and tarps and outboard motors. They must have brought everything they owned with them.

I wanted to make one of the little kids laugh. Maybe I could cheer him up a bit and he'd enjoy his trip a little more. These trips can get pretty awful sometimes. I know, I was on one once, all the way from Ottawa to Vancouver and back again.

I stuck my thumbs in my ears and let my tongue hang right out. I crossed my eyes and fanned my fingers very close to the kid's window. It just made him worse. He shoved his face into his granny's neck and started howling. The granny looked at me like I was some kind of a dog turd or something.

Dad would have made the kid laugh. I was trying to do something like Dad would do. But it didn't work.

A little further down the road I noticed a family of four up on a flat rock. There was a dad and a mum and two kids, a boy and a girl. It made me a bit lonesome. Then I saw the father was pointing out over the sea, telling them all something. Suddenly the boy threw a sandwich or something he was supposed to be eating into the water. The father saw him and grabbed his arm and shook him a bit. The kid's head was going back and forward. They looked like they were having just a wonderful time. My lonesomeness went away in a hurry.

On the little road into Peggy's Cove the traffic stopped again and the driver of another Winnebago got out and looked up and down and blew a hockey whistle. I realized we were prisoners in the middle of a convoy of Winnebagos and this guy was the signaling leader.

"Sometimes it's just like a parade!" Aunt Fay said, and we started to move again.

After about an hour of creeping along in the traffic we went down the hill into the perfect fishing village and pulled into Aunt Fay's laneway beside her shop right in front of the perfect spot where everybody wants to take the perfect picture.

Aunt Fay showed me my room and I unpacked. She had to go to her gift shop and said that I might as well go out for a little exploring.

I headed up the hill towards the lighthouse and the restaurant.

I watched the tourists pouring in and out of the door and pushing and shoving and yelling and crossing the road to go over and feel the lighthouse and look at the sea. I was busy noticing how they all looked the same when suddenly one person in the crowd looked different from the rest.

This guy was sitting along the side of the restaurant with a plastic shopping bag between his knees, carefully putting rocks in it and weighing it each time he put in another rock. He was older and taller than me and he had red hair and pimples. One of his feet was beating up and down on the grass and he was whistling.

That night, before I went to bed, I was telling Aunt Fay about the tourists and how most of them would go over to the lighthouse and put their hands on it, feel it.

"Why do they do that?" I asked.

"They want to see if it's real," she said. "Lots of people who visit here don't believe it's a real village, because it's so perfect. They think they're visiting a model of a village. They think it's a kind of museum. They peek in people's windows and sometimes wander right into your house just to look around."

"I think I saw a boy who comes from here."

"You couldn't have. There are no kids around here."

"This one was older than me but he didn't look like a tourist. He wasn't with anybody and he wasn't dressed like they were."

Aunt Fay gave me a look.

"What did he look like?"

"Taller than me, red hair, pimples. Sort of nervous looking."

"Sounds like James Drummond. He's not the type

of person your mum and dad would like you to hang around with. Doesn't come from Peggy's Cove. Comes from down the coast near Indian Harbour. Hangs around here a lot though. Not a nice boy."

That got me.

Nervous and not nice?

That was worth investigating.

3

I met him two nights later.

I was sitting at a small table in the restaurant when I realized I was listening to a drumming sound. I turned around and looked at the table behind me. It was him. He was knocking out a very fast rhythm with the fingers of one hand and beating time with his other. His foot was knocking the table leg on the off-beat.

He was staring right at me and drumming away.

"I know you," he said, "you live at the gift shop. I've seen you on the veranda."

"I'm Ryan," I said. "And you're James Drummond. My aunt told me about you."

"My friends call me Drummer."

He never took his eyes off mine. He stared right into them while we were talking. It was almost like being hypnotized. I had to look away a couple of times and pretend I was brushing a crumb or something off the table.

"I'm working the night shift this time."

"You work here?"

"All over."

"What kind of work?"

"See that plastic shopping bag with the Canadian flag on it beside that tourist's chair? I'm working on that at the moment."

The Drummer changed to a one-hand rhythm, reached down with his free hand beside his chair and lifted up a similar plastic shopping bag with a Canadian flag on it. There was another smaller satchel beside it.

"You could say I'm a fisherman — I fish the tourists. Want to work with me tonight? Go outside and get me two stones about so big." He made a shape about the size of a grapefruit with his hands. I didn't move.

"Well? Are you going?"

"What are the stones for?" I said.

"I'll tell you after you get them."

"I don't think I want to get them unless I know what they're for."

"You don't want to work with me?"

"I don't know if I do or not."

His drumming was starting to affect me. My foot was tapping with his rhythm.

"Your last chance."

"How about you get the stones and I'll watch what you do with them," I said.

"Okay, sucker. But you're missing one of life's big opportunities to work with a pro!"

Then the Drummer got up and left the restaurant, snapping his fingers and nodding his head the whole way.

I looked in his plastic shopping bag with the Canadian flag on it. Inside were empty gift boxes and crumpled-up newspaper. The other bag was on the floor beside his chair.

Back he came with the stones and set them on the table in front of him so his hands were free to play some quick tom-tom.

His eyes got very narrow and he stared at the tourist's plastic bag beside her chair. Her family were all eating and looking around while they chewed.

"That's a pretty heavy bag the way she carried it in. And she set it down nice and easy so there's glass in it probably. Maybe dishes, or maybe a piece of sculpture. Soapstone is the best. From way up in the Arctic. Some of those carvings are worth over a hundred bucks."

Then I realized what he was going to do. He was going to switch bags with the tourist.

He put his stones in newspaper and snuggled them into the gift boxes and then into the bag. He was blowing a very fast tune through his lips and his knees were going up and down like crazy.

"Now let's find out what's on top."

He got up, passed right by their table, looked out the window and came back.

"Rectangular box, wrapped in brown paper, from your aunt's shop. That's good news, expensive stuff from there, probably a hand-knit scarf or some Indian leatherwork, belt maybe."

From his other bag he pulled a collapsed rectangular box, a sheet of brown paper and a roll of Scotch tape.

He was an excellent wrapper. Corners just perfect. Obviously he'd had lots of practice.

He set the box into the top of the bag on top of the other empty boxes, newspaper and the two big stones.

"Now to test the weight."

Out of his satchel he took a small rack mounted with a dozen or so Peggy's Cove pins and miniature lighthouses and tourist stuff.

He started two tables away from where the bag was, asking if they wanted to buy a pin. They didn't want any. The next table bought one. Then he was standing with the bag between him and the lady. While he held the display of pins quite close to her face he quickly lifted the bag and moved it over a couple of inches and said excuse me or something. They said no thank you and he moved on to two or three more tables and then came back.

"Heavy, heavy bag. Need probably two more stones. This is going to be a good one!"

He looked at me while he beat out a waltz.

"You going for those extra stones?"

"Don't think so."

"Your last chance to work with a pro. Okay, sucker. Opportunity of a lifetime down the drain."

He was back with the stones and carefully re-packed his bag, wiggling and twitching and whistling softly and drumming away when his hands were free.

"It'll happen when they pay the bill."

There was the usual mob scene at the cash register. Everybody was jammed in the narrow passage, coming in, going out, paying their bill, asking questions, buying maps and post cards, fiddling with souvenirs, dropping parcels, counting money, shouting, arguing, crying, yawning, reaching up to their elbows in purses, looking for wallets, slapping kids and putting their shopping bags down on the floor beside their legs.

"Study the tourists," he said, "and you'll be a big success!" Then he joined the crowd.

The Drummer was smooth as silk. I watched him exchange the shopping bags with the Canadian flags.

I could tell by his lips he was whistling softly.

The Drummer's tourists got their bill paid, picked up their bag of empty boxes and stones and left.

The Drummer paid his bill, gave me a little show-off salute and disappeared out the door into the Peggy's Cove night-time mist.

I left the restaurant and walked over to the lighthouse. The fog was hanging over the rocks and the powerful light was cutting through it like a tunnel. I could hear the sea pounding and sucking.

I was wondering what the Drummer did with the stuff he stole. Some of it would be from Aunt Fay's shop. Maybe he took it to Halifax and sold it to somebody. Some Mafia man or somebody.

I wondered what Dad would think of this guy. What he would think about this whole thing that the Drummer did? I might just become the Drummer's partner. Dad wouldn't like it a bit. So what? If he was so concerned about my future why did he take off on me?

The Drummer and I could go into business. New tourists to steal from every day. Every day a new crop of suckers. I could be his inside man in the shop. I wouldn't steal from Aunt Fay but I could tell him when some dope bought something really expensive and we could work from there.

Then after we got successful I'd buy a big Cadillac and move to Halifax and get some other people to do the dirty work and I'd just run it from a big office in the city and I'd wear rings on all my fingers and sit behind a glass desk and Dad would show up needing a shave and bumming a dollar for a drink of booze and I'd get some of my goons to throw him down the stairs.

I went home through the fog feeling kind of rotten about throwing Dad down the stairs but feeling kind of excited at the same time.

4

The Drummer was a thief for sure. But I liked him. He had what Dad calls "style."

"Study the tourists," he had said. That's what Aunt Fay said too so that's just what I did.

I studied the tourists. I watched thousands of them go by the shop at that perfect spot in Peggy's Cove.

Right in front of the veranda where I would sit was the exact place where all the tourists wanted to take the famous picture of the cove and the sun sinking into the sea. They all want to stand in that one spot and take their very own post-card picture.

There is only one road through Peggy's Cove and the tourists start coming down that road from both ends.

There's a guy in a wheelchair wheeling himself down the road with his camera flying. He's burning rubber all the way. He wants his own picture of the perfect sunset.

There are ladies and men of all shapes and sizes and kids of all ages with their tourist outfits and their cameras all running and falling over each other and pushing each other out of the way trying to get to the spot.

The sun is touching the water and more tourists are on their way from the top of the hill.

The guy in the wheelchair swerves off the road and crashes into the rocks. Some people put him back in his chair, pull him out on the road again and send him on his way.

The bottom of the sun is in the water. Three minutes left!

A guy running with his camera around his neck falls on his face and his camera explodes in a thousand pieces. He's saying tourist words as he picks up the pieces while people step on his fingers.

Hundreds of tourists are on their way. Two minutes!

The sun is half-way in the water.

People are shoving each other off the perfect spot. There is a lady in a big floppy hat. She puts her camera to her eye. She takes a picture of her hat.

The sun is three-quarter's way into the water.

Everybody's yelling and arguing and pushing and shoving and focusing and swearing.

The tourists who can't get in front are jumping up and down taking pictures of other people taking pictures. Three tourists get pushed into the cove water and drown their cameras.

A man takes a picture of his own finger.

Little kids are screaming and crying.

The guy in the wheelchair is back in the rocks on the other side of the road. Nobody is helping him this time. He leaves his wheels there and tries to crawl the rest of the way.

There is not much time left.

The sun is just peeking out of the sea.

Aunt Fay comes out of the gift shop and stands with me on the veranda. She is ready. In a few minutes the sun will be in the water and all the tourists will turn around and jam into the shop and buy thousands of dollars worth of expensive crafts and Canadiana.

Aunt Fay is ready.

She puts her head back and laughs and makes that little lonesome dog-tied-in-the-yard-at-night sound.

Then she ducks into the shop.

In a minute I have to get out of the way because people start pouring in.

It's dangerous to be in the way when a horde of tourists decides it wants to do something!

Then I see the Drummer. He's disguised as a tourist. He's wearing three cameras. I wonder if they belong to him.

5

For that first week or so, I was really a watcher.

I watched and listened to everything.

I loved the fishermen. I watched them lift their boats up to the wharf so that they could dump the fish in the big tubs near the cutting table. I watched the parts of the fish fly up over the cutting table and the gulls attack the wharf and the tourists jump all over the place.

And I'd watch the fishermen hose down the wharf and then disappear into their fish-houses and I'd wonder where they went.

I watched the tourists, I watched the fishermen and I helped Aunt Fay in the gift shop sell all her stuff and I got out of the way when too many tourists came running and of course I thought about Dad.

I'd feel like saying a few things to him. I guess if he were there with me I'd have said very quietly:

"Remember when Grampa died? The day after the funeral I took another day off school and you bought me a knife in a sport shop on Bank Street and we were coming out of the store and you said you thought you saw Grampa going by the window just a minute ago? And we sort of ran down the street a bit and then we stopped and started walking again and you said that it was silly, we couldn't have seen him because he was gone forever? And you cried a little bit and then you said not to worry because you didn't cry at the funeral and you had to cry sometime so you might as well cry right here on Bank Street as anywhere else.

"And that was your father and you know how you felt when he went away!"

On those first few mornings I'd wake up really early, before it was light. I'd open my eyes in the black dark in my room and I'd hear a motor starting up and a bubbly frothy sound of an engine as it pulled out of the cove. Then later when there was some gray in the window I could hear another boat and then another.

It was the boats going out for their day of fishing.

This one day, I was sitting on the veranda of the shop watching the sea. It was about three in the afternoon and the last fishing boats were already in. The fish were all cleaned and the fishermen had all disappeared into their fish-houses along the wharf.

The tourists were crowding past me into the gift shop. They were pretty crabby and some of their kids were crying.

The ladies in the shop had their purses and their wallets out and the money was flying around. Aunt Fay was stuffing money into the big pockets in her dress and there was money falling on the floor and the people were buying everything they could.

Aunt Fay's black cat was asleep beside some fur mitts. A lady poked her finger into the cat and said, "How much is this?" The cat just looked at her. She bought the mitts instead. I decided I'd sat long enough and went up to the lighthouse on the point where I could watch the water smash into the rocks.

First I went into the post office at the bottom of the lighthouse to see what was going on.

The lighthouse lady was talking to some tourists while she gave them stamps.

"Yes, that's what it says. 'Warning: the ocean and rocks are treacherous.'" I knew she was talking about the iron plaque on the side of the lighthouse.

"A wave came up only last month and grabbed an American and took him away."

She was talking very quietly. When she spoke, even the tourists got a little quiet. She seemed like a very nice lady.

39

I went outside and read the plaque.

WARNING
Injury and Death
Have Rewarded Careless
Sight-Seers Here
The Ocean and Rocks Are Treacherous
Savour the Sea From a Distance

I liked the words "Rewarded" and "Savour the Sea" the best. And "Treacherous." An idea about Dad was coming into my mind. I wonder if he knew how *dangerous* it was around here!

I went down to the edge until the spray hit my face. I savoured the sea from close up.

I edged further on the rocks. I could see that every eighth wave or so came up higher than the rest. I could hear how it sucked back as it fell away. I was thinking about the American. When the big one hit and sucked away I went out as far as I could on the rock where the slime made it slippery and where the big one, six waves from now would come crashing right over me and suck me down. Five, six, seven… I backed up and stumbled a bit and got off just in time. The big one crashed down at my feet and sucked away with a horrible sound. I looked back and noticed some tourists were watching me and taking my picture.

"How's that?" I said to Dad, "How's that for danger? One more second and I would have been drowned. What do you think of that?"

Then I went back down the hill to the shop.

Things had died down a bit. The tourists wouldn't be back in big flocks until sunset.

Aunt Fay came out of the shop and sat on the veranda with me.

"Have you ever been to the top of the hill?"

"To the lighthouse?"

"No. The other way."

"No."

"See the orange house on the top of the hill?"

"Yes."

"See the lawn chair on the lawn and the man in the straw hat in the chair?"

"Yes."

"That's Eddie. He's the most important man in Peggy's Cove. He's the senior fisherman here. He sits up there every day from three to four o'clock on his lawn and relaxes after his day's work. That's his boat right out there by the wharf. The orange one. If you'd like to go up there I have something for you to give him."

41

She went into the shop.

Eddie could see the whole town of Peggy's Cove from his chair on the hill.

"He asked me to order these for him," said Aunt Fay when she came back out on the veranda. She handed me a big pair of orange fluorescent gloves.

"These are special rubberized gloves that Eddie wears to protect his hands when he's fishing. He has a very painful rash from the salt water. And he likes orange."

I started to leave with the gloves but Aunt Fay said one more thing.

"Don't ask him to take you fishing."

"Why?"

"Were you going to?"

"Yes."

"Well, don't. If you ask him he won't take you. But if you don't ask him, he will."

At the top of the hill I turned and looked back down the road. I could see Aunt Fay's shop and all the other stores and the wharf and the fish-houses and the boats tied up and some tiny tourists wandering around and a Winnebago in the ditch on the rocks and on the other side, on top of the other hill, the lighthouse and the restaurant — and most of all, the sea.

As far as you could see, the sea!

I went up to Eddie's chair.

He was looking at me out under his orange straw hat.

"My Aunt Fay sent me up with these gloves to give to you."

"Isn't that nice. Who are you?"

"Ryan."

"Ryan, is it? Isn't that nice. Let's see those gloves now. Aren't they nice! Do they fit, I wonder? Yes! Well now, they fit very nice! Nice of you to bring them up for me. Very nice!"

When I can't say what I want to say I don't say anything. I wanted to ask him if I could go out in his boat with him but I couldn't. So I just stood there like a dummy looking at the sea.

"Nice day?" Eddie said.

"Yes it is."

Some people were down in the rocks pushing the Winnebago.

"Yes, it's a very nice day," Eddie said.

The Winnebago tipped over on its side and the tourists were running all over the place. I could see the Drummer down there, "helping" everybody.

"So you're her nephew, I hear."

"Yes. Yes I am."

"Isn't that nice."

I could hear a few gulls yelling down in the cove.

"Well now, I think I'll take these nice gloves and go in and have myself a nice nap. It was nice of you to bring these up for me. And it was nice of your Aunt Fay to order them for me."

Some people were taking pictures of the wounded Winnebago. Walking the other way was the Drummer, carrying a big basket.

"Well, I'd better go now," I said.

"Yes, well, nice meeting you."

"Yes. Well. Bye."

"Bye!"

I got a little way down the hill and I heard Eddie call me. I turned around.

"I leave in the morning around five o'clock!" he shouted.

When I got back to the veranda of the shop I was out of breath. Aunt Fay was still sitting there.

"I could see you talking to Eddie."

"I gave him the gloves."

"What do you think of him?"

"He's nice," I said. "He's really nice."

6

Aunt Fay gave me an alarm clock so I could get up early and be ready for Eddie. She said the clock ticked very loud and she hoped I didn't mind. I said I didn't mind, in fact I liked loud ticking on a clock because it reminded me of my grandmother's apartment in the afternoon when everything is so quiet and the sun is making bright lights on the floor through the curtain and all you can hear is the clock.

I set it for four and went to sleep.

I always seem to wake up about one minute before an alarm goes. Dad says I have a clock in my head. I wake up but I don't open my eyes. I just put my hand out so that it's right over the clock and I wait for it to ring. It's sort of like catching a frog. You put your hand over him very slowly and lower it very slowly, then — BANG! you've got him.

The alarm went and I grabbed it. I brought it right up to my face and opened my eyes.

It said exactly *five* o'clock!

I set it wrong the night before!

I got dressed in twenty seconds, took the stairs four at a time and shot out the door.

Just then I heard a boat start. There was fog and some daylight.

I raced over the road and down to the water, ran up the ramp into the back door of the fish-house, out the sea door and onto the wharf.

Eddie's boat was just heading out of the cove. Ten seconds earlier and I could have jumped into it as it moved out!

There were two people in the boat.

Eddie was driving. I could see the back of his neck and his straw hat and his orange fluorescent gloves. He didn't turn around.

At the back of the boat the second person was looking right at me. He was standing right beside the red running-light.

I must tell you that his face looked like a turtle's face. It was very wrinkled and it came out in front in a kind of blunt snout. The eyes were away back and they looked shut except for two little lights shining there in the slits.

He was waving at me.

Then he opened his mouth wide as though he was saying something. But nothing seemed to come out.

Then the fog closed around the boat so that all I could see was the red running-light and all I could hear was the motor sounding very muffled and bubbly.

Then there was nothing.

I was so mad at myself for missing the boat I thought I could hear thunder all around.

Then I thought I didn't want to go fishing anyway. Being with the Drummer would be more fun. It would have been alright with Eddie alone. Eddie was nice. But why did he have that other ugly thing with him? Who wants to go fishing with a guy who looks like a turtle?

That afternoon I was standing near the lighthouse savouring the sea with the Drummer. I told the Drummer I might try to write my dad a letter about some of the things I was doing in Peggy's Cove and that if the letter made him sad or guilty he might decide to come home. Parents have responsibilities. They should be around to take care of their kids and see that they don't hurt themselves or get in trouble.

"It'll never work," said the Drummer.

"Why not?"

"First place, they're too smart. They see right through that stuff. Second place, I know it doesn't work because I tried it."

"Your dad took off too?"

"Two years ago. He used to hit me a lot."

"And you wrote him a letter with stuff in it that was going to make him feel sad or guilty?"

"That's right. I told him I was arrested for stealing and put on probation."

"Why did you tell him that?"

"Because it was true."

"Did he come home?"

"No. He answered my letter though."

"What did he say?" I asked.

"He said, 'Nice try.'"

"Nice try?"

"That's right. Is your dad stupid?"

"No."

"Well, neither is mine. Yours will probably say the same thing."

The gulls were sitting on the wind as though they were hanging by invisible threads.

"You need another angle. That's if you're really serious. Personally I don't think dads come back very often once they go."

"I think mine will."

48

"Why did he leave?"

"He was acting funny. I don't know."

"Well, anyway, you need something better than that guilt and sadness gimmick."

The gulls were crying, "Don't! Don't!"

I was looking right at the Drummer's eyes and watching his head bob up and down in time to some beat or other. He was scanning Peggy's Cove for suckers.

Then it hit me.

I could pretend I was involved in a life of crime — tell Dad all about it — see what kind of reaction I'd get. I'd give him a real fish story about how I was tied up with thieves and everything. He wouldn't say "nice try" like the Drummer's dad did.

I wouldn't need to actually *steal* anything; I could just go with the Drummer and say I was his partner.

That night I wrote up the whole plastic-shopping-bag-incident for Dad's letter and included myself as the Drummer's partner.

I was now a crook!

That will get him, I thought.

That night Aunt Fay was talking to me about my alarm clock.

"Maybe something's wrong with it," she said. "I'll lend you mine so you'll be sure and not miss the boat tomorrow morning."

"I don't think I'm going to go fishing." I said.

"Oh?"

"I've got other things to do."

"I don't think that's very wise."

The house was very quiet. All I could hear was Aunt Fay's fridge humming in the kitchen.

"I said, I don't think that's very wise."

I didn't answer her. I just looked down at my feet.

"I'll set the clock for you. You'd better go to bed so you'll be fresh for fishing tomorrow."

I went to bed thinking that it doesn't matter where you go, there's always somebody around to tell you what to do.

While she was fiddling with the clock and I was lying in bed Aunt Fay had quite a bit to say about the Drummer:

"Jimmy Drummond lives down the road, towards Indian Harbour. Very nervous. Always beating his fingers on tables or fences. Drumming. Drumming. Drives people crazy. Strange boy really. Not good company for anyone honest, I'm afraid."

I checked the clock just to make double sure it was right.

But I goofed it again.

My clock rang an hour early. It was three o'clock! Eddie didn't leave until five. I had two hours to get ready. When Aunt Fay says she's going to do something, she does it. When she sets a clock, she sure sets it. And when I check it, I sure check it.

I got dressed and went out on the road. I could see the shadow of the wharf and the fish-houses. The light turning in the lighthouse showed there was fog. The only sound I could hear was the sea pounding on the rocks up by the lighthouse and the water gurgling in the cove. It was hard to imagine that in a few hours this road would be filled up with thousands of people.

I went in and made some eggs and toast. When Dad and I go camping we don't like to dirty a whole lot of dishes. So I did what he always does. He puts a lot of butter in the frying pan and when it's sizzling a bit he puts a piece of bread in the pan. He lets the bread fry on one side then he turns it over with the egg lifter. While the other side of the bread is frying he puts two eggs in the pan beside it until they cook. It takes longer for the bread to cook so when the eggs are done he lifts them and turns them over onto the top of the bread. Then in the space where the eggs were he puts another piece of bread. Since the eggs are on top of the first piece of bread they cook very slowly. This gives you a chance to cook the second piece of bread on both sides. When it's done you flip it on top of the eggs and the other piece of bread and you've got a sandwich. You put some salt and pepper on top and turn off the stove.

Then you stand beside the stove and cut pieces of the sandwich off with the egg lifter and eat your breakfast. If you really want to get fancy you can dump a bunch of ketchup all over it before you dig in. Or maple syrup.

You also drink right out of the milk jug so you don't even need a glass and when you're finished the only dishes you've dirtied are the frying pan and the egg lifter. Then you just rinse out the frying pan and the egg lifter in the sink and put them away. That way, when the normal people come down for breakfast they don't even know anybody's been there.

Anyway, I ate, got dressed warm and went out on the veranda of Aunt Fay's shop and sat down to wait.

I was thinking about one camping trip I was on with Dad and how all we had with us was a can of beans and a can of potatoes, a frying pan and an ax. Dad smashed open the cans with the ax and we dumped everything into the pan. We cut two pieces of clean birchbark off a tree and used the pieces for spoons. After we ate all we could we noticed that there was *one* bean left in the pan and a little bit of juice. We were both looking at the bean and Dad said we had to share everything equally so he picked the bean out and put it on a stump and divided the bean in two with the ax very carefully. Then we ate the halves. Thinking about that was making me feel a little lonely so I decided I'd stop.

That was when I saw the man who was on the end of Eddie's boat the day before. He came around the side of Aunt Fay's house from the back somewhere.

It was getting light so I could see his turtle's face under his hat. He went over the road and down to the water, up the ramp into the back door of the fishhouse and came out the sea-door onto the wharf.

Then he put one hand on the cutting table where they cleaned the fish and stuck his snout up in the air and started waving his head back and forward. Back and forward. He made a bigger and bigger circle with his head until he looked like he was going to throw himself off the wharf into the water.

Then I heard footsteps and I saw Eddie coming down the road with his straw hat pulled down over his face and his hands in his pockets. On his belt were tied his new orange fluorescent gloves. When he got on the wharf Eddie touched the man on the shoulder and he stopped swinging his head.

They started putting boxes and gear into the boat. Eddie was handing stuff down to the other man in the boat now and he was saying things about some boxes and lines they were getting ready.

Then Eddie went to the front and started the motor. You could hear it all over Peggy's Cove, it was so quiet in the morning.

They were leaving.

What was I doing sitting here?

They were leaving!

After I fell twice I finally came out the sea-door. Eddie was untying one of the lines and the man was untying the other.

I stood there.

"Nice morning!" Eddie said, looking up at me.

"Yes, it's a nice morning," I said.

"This is Wingding," Eddie said. "His real name isn't Wingding but everybody calls him that. He's my fishing partner. He's a very nice fishing partner."

I stood there. Wingding was looking at me the way a turtle looks at you. I didn't know where to look or if I should say something.

"How do you do?" I finally said.

Wingding made a smacking noise.

"Like to come for a nice fish?" Eddie said.

Would I! Would I like to come for a nice fish! I'd like to go for a thousand nice fish! A million nice fish! All my life I dreamed of fishing on the ocean. All the

54

water you'd ever want! Would I! I opened my mouth and the best word I know came out. The perfect word for the situation.

"Yes."

I jumped into the boat and stood at the back with Wingding, and I stared at him while I tried not to stare at him. Eddie went to the front and put the engine in gear.

We went slowly out the cove through the fog. Eddie was watching over the side. The water was green. You could see the rocks just under the water right beside the boat.

The boat was moving up and down on the swell.

Suddenly we hit the first wave. We were out of the cove. Eddie revved up and we took off out to sea. The fog was all around us.

Wingding made a smacking noise and we pulled up to an orange buoy and tied up to it.

I was really curious about this Wingding.

He never talked — he just opened his mouth like a mud turtle does. The bottom of his face would open up and his eyes would close from the bottom like a turtle. Did you ever notice that most people's eyes close from the top down? Wingding's eyes closed from the bottom up. When his mouth opened you'd hear a bit of a "smack." When he did that you'd just have to imagine what he was saying even though he didn't say it.

If Eddie said, "Fine day?" to Wingding, Wingding would just open his mouth once and his wrinkles would move around and you'd hear a kind of "smack."

Just once. Then he'd close his face. Then you'd imagine that he said something like, "It sure is, Eddie" or "You betcha" or "Yessirree!" But not a word would come out.

So if you were standing in the boat and Wingding was behind you and he wanted to say something, you'd hear a "smack" and you'd know.

When I heard the smack I'd turn around and look at Wingding. When I heard the smack then all I'd hear was the sound of the water rubbing the sides of the boat and Eddie's line moving up and down.

It felt funny, waiting for a man who couldn't talk to say something.

After Eddie and Wingding had pulled in their bait net, we untied and took off again.

Soon the wind was blowing away the fog and the boat was moving up and down so much I started to feel funny.

I tried not to think of my breakfast. Or anything to eat at all.

We stopped again and Eddie lifted the heavy anchor and dropped it over the side.

Eddie and Wingding baited their hooks with squid and threw their lines overboard and started pulling in the fish.

All you could hear was the lines rubbing on the side of the boat and the water sloshing the side of the boat.

I tried to pick a place for my eyes to stare at, something that would stay still.

The fog was gone and the morning sun was sinking into the water and rising back out of it. I turned around and looked back at Peggy's Cove. The lighthouse was also sinking into the water and rising back out of it.

I closed my eyes and all I could see was my breakfast in the frying pan.

I opened my eyes and Wingding was looking at me.

He must have known.

My face probably looked green.

Wingding put his hand on my arm and gave me a line and pointed to the bait box. He lifted up a squid and gave it to me.

I cut up the squid just like Eddie and Wingding did and it squirted black thick juice on my wrist.

I felt my throat come up. Please God don't let me be sick. Please!

I threw in my line and let it down. Watching the line made me feel better. Watching where the line went into the water made me stop thinking about my breakfast.

Eddie and Wingding were pulling in fish and filling the boxes. I was starting to feel a little better. I imagined my face was only gray now and not green.

All of a sudden everything stopped. The fish stopped biting. Eddie and Wingding pulled in their lines.

As I started to do the same I got a bite. I pulled and pulled and finally lifted it out of the water.

Anything too small, then Eddie and Wingding would throw it back in the water and about 500 gulls would fight over it until one of them got it.

My fish was small. It was as wide as it was long, but small.

Eddie and Wingding were resting, leaning on the side of the boat, watching me.

I stood there holding up this stupid-looking square fish.

"Isn't that nice?" Eddie said and Wingding smacked a bit.

I started taking it off the hook.

"Keep your thumb away from his mouth or he'll give you a nice bite!" Eddie said.

The fish looked like a turnip with a mouth and about a hundred horns all around his body and a stupid little tail that other fish must have laughed at.

I threw him back in the water.

The gulls hit the water the same time my turnip did. Suddenly they all started yelling and crabbing at each other. Then they all looked at my fish. Not one of them would even try it. My first fish. The gulls didn't even want it!

Wingding put his hand on my shoulder and made a smacking noise.

Then we lifted anchor and went to the next spot further out to sea.

It was seven o'clock in the morning.

7

After a few trips out I got to be the third best fisherman in the boat. Eddie was the best. Wingding was the second best. I was the third best.

That sounds funny, I know. There were only three of us, so being the third best is almost like saying I was the worst. But I don't mean that. I mean that I was almost as good as Wingding at catching fish and Wingding was almost as good as Eddie and Eddie was the best fisherman, I think, on the whole planet Earth. I also think that if somebody else had come along to fish with us I wouldn't have all of a sudden been fourth. Maybe *that* person would have been fourth.

I knew I was getting pretty good because I was imitating Eddie.

I tried to do everything Eddie did. That's the best way to learn anything. If you want to learn something, find somebody who's really good at it and copy him. Do *everything* he does. Act the way he does. Wear the same clothes as he does. Talk the way he does. Walk the way he does. Then you'll be good too.

If Eddie put his feet a certain way when he stood in the boat, I'd put my feet exactly the same way. If Eddie put his straw hat on his head a certain way, I'd do the same with my hat. Whatever way Eddie would put his face, I'd put mine the same way.

There was one thing that took me quite a while to learn. Just before Eddie jerked his line to set the hook, he'd turn his head and look away out to sea over the other side of the boat. He looked like he was trying to *listen* to his fish. And he also looked like he was pretending he didn't care if there was a fish there or not. He looked like a quarterback does when he's looking one way and then all of a sudden throws the ball the other way where he wasn't looking at all.

Whenever Eddie did that, you knew that about two seconds later his arm would fly up until the orange fluorescent glove was high in the air, and then he'd start to haul with both hands. Hand over hand, fast at first, the gloves would be a kind of orange blur, then slower when his catch came near the top. When it was almost at the top, Eddie would stop hauling and take a look. Then, in a very nice way, he'd lift the fish out of the water, tear it off the hook, throw it over his shoulder right into the box without looking.

And another thing. As soon as he made his first pull, just when his orange fluorescent glove was high in the air, he'd somehow know what kind of fish he had. Up would go the glove and Eddie would say "cod" or "haddock" and he'd be right every time. That was the hardest part. That was the part I couldn't learn. I would just guess.

If you want to know how big the hook was that we used, look at the finger that you say "come here" with. The hook was about that big. For weights Eddie used a heavy silver bar that was attached to the line above the hook.

We usually fished in very deep water.

Imagine being on the ninth floor of an apartment building. Go out on the balcony with your strong nylon line with the silver bar and the "come here" hook attached. Throw the bar over the side and let the line run through your hands until the bar hits bottom. Then pull it back up so that the hook is just off the lawn. Look down. It's a long way.

Suddenly there's a new weight on the end! A weight that's alive and pretty mad and that doesn't want to come up to the ninth floor on the balcony with you.

So you start hauling. Hand over hand. One floor,

two floors, three, four, your arms are getting tired, five, six, you've got to keep the line tight or it will jerk and you'll lose your catch, seven, eight, your arms are getting numb, eight and a half, just a bit more, now stop, look, now nicely lift him over the railing and you've got him.

Do that fifty times and you know what it's like fishing with Eddie.

8

Funny how if you do something often and you start to try and remember each time you did it, you can't. All those times start to seem like one time.

If you walk down the same street to go to school about a million times, you can't remember each time. You can only remember maybe the first time and then all the other times bunch up into one.

For instance, I'm remembering Wingding. He sits on the edge of the boat as quiet and still as he can with this big grin on him and he's waiting.

When Eddie catches a cod that's too small and tears it off the hook and throws the cod over his shoulder and it lands in the water right beside the boat, about a thousand gulls come to grab it and fight over it screaming and yelling "Don't! Don't!"

And Wingding is sitting there on the edge of the

boat with this grin on him and his face is a kind of red-dish-blue color like he's holding his breath. And then when the gulls get finished fighting over the little cod and come and sit on the boat to watch what Eddie's going to do, one of them sits right behind Wingding's bum on the edge of the boat.

Wingding is leaning over as still as can be and his face is red now because he hasn't breathed in about a half an hour.

Suddenly Wingding just about rips his pants with a huge long fart that sounds like a tent ripping.

And it blows the gull right off the edge of the boat and the gull starts yelling "Don't! Don't!" and Wingding falls to the floor of the boat and starts laughing and while he's laughing he's rolling around in the fish slime and squid pieces and blood and lines and goo is squirting out under him while he goes "smack."

And that Eddie, he just keeps pulling in the cod and throwing the big ones on top of Wingding…

And I'm remembering the cod.

A cod is a reddish brown color and has big bulgy eyes and a big mouth. A cod looks like a man named Frank who Dad used to bring home to our place sometimes. He had a great big mouth and sharp pointy teeth and big bulging eyes.

And Dad said you could tell what Frank was thinking and what he was going to say just by staring at him.

A cod is the same. You can tell what he's thinking if you just stare at him for a while. Of course, you can't tell what he's going to say, because a cod doesn't say much.

I used to try it with my dad's friend Frank and it usually worked.

I'd stare at him and all of a sudden, for instance, I could tell he was going to start to sing. Then all of a sudden he'd open his mouth and you could see his tongue and his pointy teeth and his eyes would start to pop out even more and his face would get a kind of blue color and he'd start singing.

Or he'd be at our place for supper and Mum would be kind of mad and I'd stare at Frank and I'd know he was going to say "pass the butter." Then right away he'd say "pass the butter" and Dad would have to reach over and get it because it was away over beside Mum but she wouldn't pass it to Frank because he wasn't invited over for supper in the first place.

Anyway, every time Eddie'd pull up a cod I'd think of Dad's friend Frank and his bulgy eyes.

I told Eddie about Frank and how he sang and everything and Eddie looked at me and told me that when he was a kid out fishing with his dad a long time ago, his dad caught a cod who could sing "Oh Canada!" and his dad took it and ran away to the circus with it and never came back.

"Wasn't that nice," Eddie said.

Dads seem to run away a lot!

And I'm remembering the wharf.

If you ever want to see the air full of fish heads and guts and backbones and skins and tails, go and watch Eddie and the rest of them cleaning their catch on the wharf at Peggy's Cove.

"That Wingding," Eddie would say, "that Wingding can clean a fish faster'n better'n nicer than any man livin' today! And that's a fact!"

And soon as the cleaning started it was a race to see who got there first, the gulls or the tourists.

First Eddie would stand up to the cutting table and get his knife going. Then the gulls would close in and start screaming. At the same time the tourists would start pushing and shoving their way on the wharf and Eddie would start throwing the heads and stuff near their legs to keep them back and keep them from asking a whole lot of dumb questions.

But some of them would get close enough anyway.

"Does the ocean freeze in the winter?"

"Did you ever catch a whale?"

"Is a squidjigging a very big fish?"

Then maybe an American would start yelling: "Hey, Martha! Come on over and stand beside this fisherman here while I grab a photo." And Martha would say, "My he's perfect, isn't he?"

"Hey, over here," somebody else would say, pointing at me, "this must be his grandson... Are you a fisherman too, sonny? Do you like being a fisherman?"

Then somebody else might say something to Wingding but he'd just "smack" at them and offer them a fish head and a handful of guts and that would be the end of *that* conversation.

Then somebody else would say to Eddie, "Do the fish suffer much? Does it hurt to catch them?"

"Not unless you cut your fingers on the teeth or on the horns. And that's not very nice."

"No, I mean do the *fish* suffer?"

"Oh the fish," Eddie would say. "Well, I don't know about *every* fish but I know a haddock will often cry and beg and pray when you first pull him out of the water. Funny thing about the haddock, the tears are fresh, not salty, like ours."

"Oh my, that's sad."

"Nice of you to say so."

"Pardon?"

"I said, 'Nice day, don't you think so?'"

"Yes, a very nice day. Nice boat you have."

"Nice of you to say so."

Just then, Wingding heaves a fish head at me across the wharf and it's got quite a few bloody strings hanging from it and the tourists have to duck and the conversation is over.

Then Eddie is tired and it's Wingding's turn. Wingding smacks and steps up to the table. You can see his knife flashing in the sun. The air is full of heads and parts of haddock and cod. There's so much in the air that the gulls don't even land — they pick their dinners out of the air — and the faster Wingding goes the more the tourists back off the wharf. Now you can't see Wingding at all. Just a cloud of fish-parts.

You can just hear Eddie laughing and saying, "Isn't this nice?" and Wingding smacking and the tourists saying things like, "Come on Martha," and "Watch, don't step in that" and "Let's go and buy something!"

Then the gulls are full and we salt the cod for the barrel and weigh the haddock and hose down the wharf and head for home.

So my mornings were really busy and I always felt great.

But the afternoons, they were a whole other story.

In the afternoons I'd go looking for the Drummer. It was a funny thing but when I'd find him and watch him do some of his tricks on the tourists, that night I wouldn't be able to talk to Aunt Fay about very much. We'd sit there and have our supper and just say small things about the weather and the shop and stuff. But when I couldn't find the Drummer, Aunt Fay and I would have long talks at supper time and we'd laugh and tell stories about Dad and crack jokes and be really good friends.

The Drummer's tricks were pretty good. I read a story once called The Master Thief. In it, the guy could steal an egg right out from under a bird in the nest. The Drummer was like that.

We'd stand on the side of the road with a board full of souvenirs of Peggy's Cove. The Drummer would sell them cheap. He didn't make money on the souvenirs. He'd make it in other ways. Mostly with kids. The tourists would sometimes send their kids out of the car with some money to buy a lighthouse or lobster-trap trinket. The Drummer would always make sure they were leaving Peggy's Cove, not coming in. He'd sell the kid some stuff and give him too much change. Then he'd say, kind of quiet so the parents wouldn't hear, "Better get your dad to count that to see if it's right." When the honest dad would find out he'd usually send the kid back with the extra money and tell the Drummer to keep it.

Sometimes the Drummer would have to go up to

the car and be real charming and make the change himself again, and this time shortchange the tourist a big amount if the bills were big. Like five dollars. Because now the dad felt so honest and nice he'd forget to check. The Drummer would fold up the change and give it back to the dad in a very sincere manner and start talking about their trip and giving them directions and sort of pushing and patting their car to send them on their way.

And away they'd go, happy.

In his other hand the Drummer would have the five.

I would be holding the board of souvenirs.

Some days he'd have a tire pump and wait outside the restaurant to help people with flat tires. If their campers were parked right close to the building it was easy to let the air out of a tire without anybody seeing you.

That was my job.

The Drummer would refuse to take any money. Then they'd offer him more. Then he'd take it.

I'd hold the pump while he took the money.

Those nights, during supper, Aunt Fay and I would be almost silent.

The Drummer could steal cameras and binoculars too. Sometimes he'd cut the straps with a short pair of sharp scissors if the tourist had tied his camera to his rearview mirror while he was parked or his binoculars to a railing while he was taking a picture.

And there was his fish trick. Tourists love to buy fresh fish. If they wanted halibut, the Drummer would sell them salted cod and tell them it was halibut. If they wanted haddock, the Drummer would sell them salted cod and tell them it was haddock. If they asked for swordfish, the Drummer would sell them salted cod and tell them it was swordfish.

Salted cod is only worth half of what those other fish are worth.

And besides, the Drummer would steal the salted cod from the fishermen's barrels at night.

But his plastic shopping bag trick was the best. When he did that one I'd always think of the Master Thief and the bird in the nest.

One morning I mentioned the Drummer to Eddie and Wingding. I didn't say much about him. I just mentioned him. Eddie started talking in an irritated kind of voice. I had never heard him grumpy before. He said a whole lot of things, like he would never take the Drummer fishing because the Drummer was too nervous. He jumped around too much. He wasn't safe in a boat. He might get all tangled up in the lines. He might get hurt. Eddie'd like to take him but he couldn't;

too bad. It'd be nice if he could come but…well, the Drummer was just too jumpy…nice boy mind you…but too twitchy to be in a boat…could cause an accident…too bad; nice boy though; a real wiggler…never seen anybody like him…like a fly in a bottle he is.

He didn't say anything about the Drummer stealing from tourists or stealing the salt cod. I wonder if Eddie even knew.

I felt pretty ashamed after he was finished. This boat was not a proper place even to say the Drummer's name. Maybe this boat was even too nice a place for a crook's helper like me to be.

Wingding just looked at me while Eddie was talking.

He didn't smack or anything.

Maybe Wingding knew.

9

Behind Aunt Fay's house there's a one-room schoolhouse that Eddie used to go to when he was a kid and that Eddie's old mother used to go to when *she* was a kid. There's a small stage at one end of the room where probably Eddie's mother used to be in plays years and years ago. In the middle of the room there's an old stove.

Aunt Fay let Wingding stay there.

"Wingding can stay there as long as he keeps it clean and doesn't smoke in bed," Aunt Fay told me.

There's only one light in the schoolhouse and it's right over the stage at one end of the room.

Wingding had his bed on the little stage right under that light.

At night he'd take off his boots and his pants and his shirt, then stand in front of his bed in his long underwear and his hat and make a big bow. Then he'd jump into bed, lie out flat under the covers, put his hands over his chest and close his eye-holes so his hat moved down over his face. Then he'd sleep.

In the morning he was in the very same position.

One night I was sitting up having tea with Aunt Fay and she was telling me a Peggy's Cove story about Widow Weed.

Widow Weed was a widow, because her husband, Mr. Weed, went out fishing in the fog about four years ago and never came back.

They found his boat later with a dead shark in it and no Mr. Weed.

They think that what he did was he brought a shark into his boat and started home and some way the shark knocked him out of his boat in the fog and the boat kept going and left him there in the water and he drowned.

"'Never bring a shark into your boat,' the fishermen all say," Aunt Fay said.

Then she told me that the Widow Weed watches the ocean every day for about an hour, then goes into her garage and talks to the shark's skull that she has nailed to the wall there.

That made me sad and I wanted to change the subject so I asked her if she wanted to go and watch Wingding's play.

She didn't know what I meant at first but then she caught on and came with me.

We went out the back door and walked through the thick night-fog to the schoolhouse.

We stood and looked through the window, with our hands beside our eyes. Wingding was on his stage in his bed.

"Let's go in and sit down," I whispered.

We went into the schoolhouse and sat down on two chairs as quietly as we could. There he was, his hat over his face and his hands over his chest.

We sat there for a long time.

Then, by mistake, I made a little noise with my chair.

Wingding's hat moved.

Then he turned his head and saw us.

Then he threw off his covers and jumped up and stood in front of his bed and started to bow!

Then Aunt Fay started to clap and so did I.

Wingding kept bowing. We started clapping louder. The louder we clapped the faster he bowed.

Then we stood up and Aunt Fay started yelling, "Bravo!" and "Encore!"

Wingding was bowing like crazy and getting in and out of bed and dropping his hat and bowing and getting back in bed and jumping up again.

We stood there clapping and yelling until our hands were sore and our throats were hoarse and Wingding was played right out.

Then Wingding flopped down on his bed, pulled up his covers, closed his eye-holes and put his hands over his chest.

On our way back to the house the fog was so thick I could hardly see Aunt Fay even though she was right beside me. But I could hear her laughing like that little dog and I knew she must be putting her head back the way she does.

10

The next afternoon I was with the Drummer.

When I came off the wharf he was there on the road, nodding and tapping and winking. I went to the house and took off my rubber boots and changed my shirt. When I came out, the Drummer was up the road a bit, walking easy so I could catch up. He was wearing a fancy chain on his belt with a watch on it that he showed me. I didn't ask him where he got it.

He was carrying a small box, gift-wrapped. I recognized the wrapping Aunt Fay used in her shop. Sometimes she'd gift-wrap stuff for people with special requests. Somebody wasn't going to get their present. I asked him what was in the box.

"How would I know?" he said with a little laugh.

"Anyway, it's for my mother. Give them a present every little while. Keeps them happy. Want to come and watch?"

"Watch what?"

"Watch me give her the present."

We walked up the road past Eddie's house. He was in his chair with his hat pulled down over his eyes. I was hoping he wouldn't look up and see me with the Drummer. We were almost past him when he looked up from under his hat. He didn't wave or anything and neither did I.

Up the road out of Peggy's Cove a couple of kilometers we came to the Drummer's house. It was a huge place with three pillars in front and a long circular driveway and a perfect lawn and a guy working on the hedges.

We went in the front door through the pillars. Inside was very cool and quiet. The rugs were thick and there was a big clock tocking at the bottom of a long set of stairs.

We went into the living room. The Drummer's mother was sitting at a huge black piano. Everything else in the room was white. White rugs, white walls, white furniture, white flowers, white telephone, white curtains. And the black piano.

"Aren't you going to introduce me to your young

friend?" the Drummer's mother said before we were even half-way into the room.

"Mother, this is Ryan. He lives in the cove with his aunt, who runs the shop there. I was just at the gift shop and bought you a present.

"Oh, how thoughtful of you, James! What is it?"

"Open it and see."

"And did your friend here help you pick it out?" She was looking at me but she was talking to him.

"No I didn't," I said. "He picked it out all by himself."

"Isn't that just lovely, James. Isn't he a thoughtful boy?" She was looking at him but she was talking to me.

"Isn't he a thoughtful son?" She was staring straight at him.

"Yes, I guess he is," I said.

She started picking at the wrapping. Her fingers were very skinny and her hands were shaking.

"My, my, what a thoughtful son." Her hands were shaking worse than ever.

The Drummer tugged me by the elbow and we went through an archway into a large kitchen with microwave ovens and fireplaces and copper pots hanging all around. We made two peanut butter and jam sandwiches and took them back into the big white

80

room with the black piano. The Drummer's mother was back sitting at the piano. The present was sitting on top of the piano in front of her. It wasn't opened. She was staring at it. We stood there and watched her for a while and then the Drummer gave me a sign with his eyes and we left.

We walked back out the circular driveway past the guy working on the hedge.

"I didn't know you were so rich." I said.

"My mother's one of the richest people in Nova Scotia. She's afraid to open that present. They say she's half crazy."

"Why do her fingers shake so much?"

"Because she's half crazy."

We walked back into town and past a mob of tourists crowded around Eddie's gate taking pictures of him in his chair.

By the time we got to the lighthouse there were so many tourists you could hardly move.

The Drummer lifted a whole box of stuff out of somebody's Winnebago.

I picked up a camera and a pair of expensive binoculars and gave them over to the Drummer. Then I went home.

That night Aunt Fay and I had a very quiet supper together.

11

Eddie had a radio and a CB on his boat. He always played the CBC on his ordinary radio and had his CB on the fisherman's channel.

What I wanted to tell Dad in the letter was how Eddie would quit fishing right when the two o'clock signal came on. I know about the two o'clock signal because I always listen to the CBC. At Peggy's Cove they get the same signal as the one we get in Ottawa, except Ottawa gets it at one o'clock. This signal has been on the radio for years and years. Even back when Dad was a kid. Dad never liked the signal. He always said that it made him nervous. He said that when he used to hear it, it meant he was going to be late for school. And that meant he'd have to go to the principal and the principal would get him in a little room behind his office and torture him by doing things like stapling his fingers to the desk and stuff.

Anyway when we're in the car and the CBC is on, Dad usually pushes some other button to try and get some rock and roll on and then he starts switching stations every time an ad for Colonel Sanders or something comes on. Then he taps his fingers on the dash and keeps time with the music.

Then I switch back to the CBC to see if there's a science program or something. There's interesting stuff on the CBC.

Dad says he's tired of hearing people discuss things. He says he likes songs with real stupid words and then he doesn't have to think. Then he switches stations again.

When he does that I sometimes turn on my CB and flip around the channels to see if there are any disasters.

CBers love disasters. That's all we ever talk about. Of course there never *are* any disasters around Ottawa.

But we talk about *maybe* disasters. I'm about the youngest one on the air. Most CBers are about Dad's age. I usually ask somebody the time or what his "20" is. Then I ask if there are any storms or tornadoes or hurricanes or floods or earthquakes or explosions or fifty car pile-ups but there never are.

All that's ever happened since I got my CB is some guy's rad boiled over on the Queensway, and everybody talked about it for about half an hour!

83

Anyway, every day on Eddie's boat we would listen to the two o'clock signal on the regular radio and wait for the long dash because that's when Eddie always said, "Time to quit" and we'd pull up our lines and head for home.

At about one minute to two the announcer would start "...and at the beginning of the long dash it will be two o'clock. Beep Beep...Beep...Beeeeep!"

"Nice time to quit!" Eddie would say.

And we would.

And that's the way it went. Eddie and Wingding and I fished in the morning. We'd finish at two o'clock every day and by about three o'clock our catch would be cleaned and Wingding would go into the fish-house out of the sun and have a little snooze and Eddie would go up the hill and sit in his chair for an hour and watch the town.

Aunt Fay told me never to bother Eddie or Wingding in the afternoons unless they invited me. I never saw Wingding in the afternoons after he went into the fish-house. Except for fishing, and the night we were uninvited guests at his play, I only saw him through my window, on his stage in the schoolhouse at night. Aunt Fay said she thought he went for walks along the highway or did odd jobs chopping wood for people in the afternoon.

84

One day when I was hanging around I looked up at Eddie in his chair and saw him waving to me to come up.

It was a hard job getting up the road to Eddie's because the tourists were so thick. At the top of the hill in front of Eddie's there was a huge crowd hanging around his gate staring at him and taking pictures of him. Eddie opened his gate for me and pulled me inside and shut it quickly before some tourists sneaked in with me. Tourists will go anywhere, whether they are invited or not. Some of them were hanging over his gate shaking cameras at us. They seemed mad.

"Worse than gulls," Eddie said.

We walked out on the point where the Widow Weed was standing. The wind was blowing her black dress. She had her arms folded. She was watching the sea.

"The Widow Weed wants to invite us for a nice cup of tea," Eddie told me.

We waited behind her a bit until she was finished. Then she turned around and we walked over to her house.

She was a lovely lady, the Widow Weed. She had very rough hands and a very soft face. And she smelled homemade. She smelled like buns cooking in the oven.

While she was in the kitchen making the tea I could hear her talking to herself.

When the tea was made we sat down for a minute in her little parlor. Then she stood up and she invited us out to her garage.

"Would you like to carry your tea?" she asked.

"That would be nice," Eddie said.

The garage was small and neat and just as clean as her house. We went in and stood with our tea and looked up at the shark's skull mounted on the wall.

"You're the one. Aren't you! You are the one. Eh? Aren't you the one!" said the Widow Weed to the shark's skull. "Aren't you the one, now? Eh? *Aren't* you the one? You're the one, aren't you now?" She was speaking very quietly.

Then she put her hand on my shoulder and looked from the shark's skull down at me. "The ocean can be very treacherous. Savour the sea from a distance!" she said.

"Isn't this nice," said Eddie.

After she talked to the shark on the wall a little more, we left the garage and Eddie and I walked back to his chair.

He sat down and pulled his straw hat down over his eyes so he couldn't see the tourists taking his picture.

I went back out his gate and walked down the hill.

Some tourists walked along beside me and asked me a whole lot of questions about Eddie and who he was and everything.

"He's my dad," I said. I didn't mind the lie.

Then I stopped to watch some people trying to pull a trailer out of the rocks along the road.

Some of them wanted to push it backwards, some wanted to go forwards. Everybody was pushing but the trailer wasn't going anywhere.

I thought a lot about the plaque on the lighthouse. And old Mr. Weed and the shark and everything, and especially about the word "treacherous."

Fishing could be treacherous. A person could get hurt or even killed, fishing. And here I am, fishing everyday in the treacherous sea.

My letter seemed really clear now.

I'd make him sad by reminding him of old times.

I'd make him worried because I was a crook.

I'd make him scared because of all the danger around.

"What do you think of that?" I said.

There were thousands of people all around me.

But I was alone.

87

12

In the evening sometimes I'd go up the hill to the restaurant by the lighthouse and have a bowl of hot raisin gingerbread and cream, which was their specialty. I would wait to see if the Drummer was going to show up.

I'd eat the hot raisin gingerbread and cream very slowly and watch the other people eat. There'd be a few tourists left and a few people from Peggy's Cove there.

Tourists don't really eat while they're eating. First of all they don't look at the person they're sitting with at the table. Whether it's their wife or their sister or their kids or something, they never seem to look at them the way normal people do.

Tourists are always looking around at people at other tables to see what they got to eat or to see what somebody's ordering or what somebody else is wearing.

Normal people look around too but not like tourists do. Tourists look around while they're chewing their food. Real people look around when they're not chewing just to see somebody interesting or to take a rest. Tourists always look like somebody's going to take away their food or hit them over the head when they're not looking.

I'd be doing a lot of planning, sitting there in the restaurant. Planning what I'd put in Dad's letter. Planning what I'd write that night in my room.

I was planning to remind Dad of the time we drove down to the Ottawa River Parkway for a "pep-talk."

"Remember the time you took me out for a little chat after I got that terrible report card? We drove down to the Ottawa River Parkway?

"It was a beautiful evening in the fall and we were sitting there in the car talking about school and all of a sudden two Mountie cars pull up one on each side and tell us to get out? And so we get out and one of the Mounties asks me if I know this man and he points at you? And it turns out that they are looking for some guy that's been attacking boys around there and then they say we'd better move along?

"And you say, What for? and there's a big argument and you say, If you've established that I'm not some sex-crazed maniac is it alright if I sit here with my son and have a chat with him this beautiful fall evening about his horrible report card?"

I told Eddie I was putting that in my letter to Dad and Eddie thought it was very nice.

"That's very nice," Eddie said. "I was seven years in that school. Right in that schoolhouse where Wingding lives."

Wingding smacked a bit when he heard his name.

"Seven years. They gave me the same report card each year. Nice way to save paper."

Anyway I'd sit there planning with my bowl of gingerbread and cream and in between, I'd sneak little peeks at the people eating, especially the people who liked each other. I guess I was a bit lonesome because of Dad and everything.

I'd look for the real people who look at each other across the table and talk about things in a quiet way and never look around when they're chewing.

One of the first times I ever went to the restaurant, I saw Eddie come in with the lady who ran the post-office. They came in and sat down away off in a corner. I couldn't see them very well so I moved my bowl over a bit and ducked my head so I could see them between a post and a big grandfather clock that was there.

They were the best eaters in the whole place. They were eating hot gingerbread and cream the same as I was — I could tell by the spoons and the bowls. Eddie would take a spoonful and the lady would take a spoonful and they'd put the spoons in their mouths at the same time. Then they'd put down the spoons and they'd chew for a while and look at each other the whole time. After they swallowed the gingerbread, they'd sit back and take a look around but you couldn't tell they were in a restaurant when they looked around. They might have been sitting on a rock or a wharf just watching the gulls or the sea. Everything was really peaceful when all of a sudden about a thousand tourists rushed the door and spoiled everything.

Tourists didn't normally arrive in mobs after the sun went down, mainly because there was no chance to take their favorite picture.

But now and then you'd get a convoy of them lost or behind schedule or something and they'd pour into Peggy's Cove to see the lighthouse at night and hit the restaurant for one last snack.

The leader came in first and put his hands on his hips and checked out the whole restaurant. You could tell he wasn't in a very good mood. His face looked very tight.

He looked like a teacher I had once who said this to a bunch of us who weren't paying attention: "If you don't shut up we'll take POETRY!"

Anyway, once the head tourist looked the place over for seats and stared at some people who were almost finished their gingerbread and cream and who were taking up whole tables by themselves (like me for instance), he went back out the door and yelled something.

Then they poured in.

Just as they jammed the door I saw Eddie and the lady gulp down the last spoonful of gingerbread, grab their stuff, wave at the cashier and get out the door sideways just in time.

In about ten seconds the place was jammed. The five of them who wanted my table were standing right beside me staring at my bowl. There was the mother and father, a granny and gramp and a kid about my age.

In the rest of the restaurant you could hear tables moving, chairs falling over, dishes breaking, people yelling and kids crying.

The kid in my group had his lips all curled up and he looked like he was either going to puke or cry. The grampa was sighing. The father was smiling. It wasn't really a smile though. It was something different from a smile. My grandfather, who is dead now, used to say it this way: "He had a grin on him like a jackass eatin' thistles!"

Just as I was moving sideways, trying to get by them, the kid said something to me I'll never forget. Nobody heard him except me.

"Are you all by yourself?" he said.

"Yes," I said.

"Geez!" he said, "are you ever *lucky*!"

Imagine! He said I was lucky because I was all by myself!

Then the Drummer came in and pulled the plastic bag trick so smoothly that I almost didn't notice.

When I got the stones for him he said, "One of life's big opportunities, this is, to work with a pro."

I was working with him. But just so I could get Dad worried. I wasn't really a crook!

"Am I really a crook?" I said out loud.

13

We fished and we fished and we pulled in thousands of pounds of cod and hundreds of pounds of haddock and we used thousands of squid for bait and we talked. And on the shore the tourists clogged up the road trying to go everywhere at once and the gulls and the sunshine filled the air and the Widow Weed watched.

We'd be about five kilometers out, just sitting there anchored, watching the lighthouse go up and down, just listening to our lines rubbing and singing on the edge of the boat.

And Eddie would do his little move and say "cod" or "haddock" and his orange gloves would start flashing in the sun, and up would come a cod or a haddock just like he said it would. And Wingding would smack or rip one at a gull.

And we'd sometimes get into little arguments about

things we happened to be talking about just to tease Wingding a bit and make him look back and forwards at us like somebody watching a tennis game. Each time he'd look at one of us he'd go "smack!"

We'd talk about things like this:

"If the groundhog sees his shadow it means a very nice short winter," Eddie would say.

"Smack!" Wingding would say.

"No, I think it's if he sees his shadow it will be six more weeks of winter," I would say.

"Smack!" says Wingding.

"Maybe you're right," Eddie would say, "if he sees his shadow it means a long winter, not very nice."

"Smack!"

"No," I'd say, "I think you're right, it means a very nice short winter."

"Smack!"

"No, I think *you're* right."

"Smack!"

"No, *you* are!"

"Smack!"

"No, I think *you* are."

"Smack!"

"Cod!"

"Smack!"

Or we might be talking about clocks.

95

"When you put the clocks ahead, you lose an hour and this makes the days nice and long," Eddie would say.

"Smack!"

"No, I think it's when you put the clocks *back* you save an hour and make the days nice and long," I would say.

"Smack!"

"Maybe you're right," Eddie would say. "If you put the clock *back*, then you get up earlier and the day is longer."

"Smack!"

"No," I'd say, "I think you're right. Put it ahead, then it's later at night but it's still daylight."

"Smack!"

"No, I think you've got it figured out very nice," Eddie'd say.

"Smack!"

"I think *you're* right."

"Smack!"

"No, you are."

"Smack!"

"Haddock!"

"Smack!"

Then we'd pull up anchor and move on a bit. And Eddie would as usual worry about the way Wingding pulled up the anchor.

"Don't lean over so far. You don't need to watch it come up. It'll come up very nice by itself. I don't like the way he leans over like that. It's not a nice way to act while you're lifting an anchor."

"Smack!" Wingding would say, leaning away out over the boat watching the anchor being winched up, his face almost touching the water.

14

About three weeks after the first fishing trip Aunt Fay asked me if I wanted to invite Eddie and Wingding over after fishing for some refreshments.

It would be around three o'clock and fairly hot so she suggested gin and lemonade and sandwiches. She was going to Halifax that morning and she'd bring back the gin and the juice and the meat for the sandwiches.

So instead of Wingding going into the fish-house for his snooze and Eddie heading up the hill to his chair, they both came over to Aunt Fay's lawn behind the shop and we had a picnic.

Aunt Fay brought out a big bottle of gin and a jug of lemonade and a plate of sandwiches and three glasses. She also had a small pail of ice cubes.

She told me to entertain my guests on the lawn.

There would be lots of gin left because it was a big bottle so she told me to put the gin up in my room after and keep it there for anytime that I wanted to entertain my guests.

We were behind the shop where the tourists couldn't see us so we were safe.

I filled my glass with ice and lemonade and handed the jug to Eddie. He put some ice in his glass, then some gin, then some lemonade. Then he picked up a sandwich and took a bite out of it.

Wingding took the glass and filled it up with gin. Then he took a sandwich and stuck the corner of it in the gin and started eating.

We talked a little bit about the Widow Weed and the shark's head and a little bit about Aunt Fay's shop and the nice stuff she had for sale in there.

Wingding was finished his sandwich and his gin. He smacked and poured himself another full glass of gin.

I was telling them about the kind of fishing I used to do with Dad and the kind of fish we used to get, like pickerel and pike and then Wingding poured himself another full glass of gin.

Soon Eddie said he had to go and it was just Wingding and me left. Wingding got hungry all of a sudden and ate all the sandwiches and poured another full glass of gin.

I was telling him more about the stuff I had put in Dad's letter.

I told him how I wrote about how dangerous it was fishing and what a smooth crook I was.

I told him how much I missed Dad, too, and how I'd sometimes pretend he was in Peggy's Cove with me in the restaurant eating some cream and gingerbread or maybe just walking down the road.

And I told Wingding how I'd pretend I was looking for Dad or I was supposed to meet him at the Careless Tourists sign. Or I'd imagine that I'd bump into him just by accident when I was going around a building or going through a door.

Then if nobody was looking I'd sort of stop and we'd have a little chat. I'd imagine Dad's face like it was before he ran away. The way he'd put his head on one side and make his eyes soft when he'd be listening to me saying something.

We'd talk about the fun we used to have at home when he'd be taking a bath and I'd wait till the bathroom was all hot and full of steam and then I'd open and close the bathroom door and work it like a fan and he'd start yelling "Help! Help! Somebody's fanning the bathroom door when I'm taking a bath! Help! Police! They're fanning the door on me again!"

After I told Wingding about fanning the door he

looked real sad. He poured the last of the big bottle of gin into his glass and he put his hand on my arm and let some tears out of his eyes and smacked a few times, very sad.

I was going to put my hand on top of his but for some reason I didn't. I still think about that. I should have put my hand on his. You should always put your hand on somebody's hand when he puts it on your arm like that. Specially if he's crying. Because if you don't, and if he dies soon after you'll be sorry. And there'll be nothing you can do about it the rest of your life.

Nothing.

Wingding pointed at the empty gin bottle lying on the grass and smacked a few times and got up and left. He went around the shop and walked down the road.

I was watching a bunch of tourists following him and running in front of him trying to talk to him and take his picture when my Aunt Fay came out of the shop and told me the news.

Mum had phoned. She had Dad's address.

I could mail my letter now.

I looked up the road towards the lighthouse. Wingding was posing for pictures. There was a big mob around him. He was bowing and taking off his hat. The tourists were going wild.

I got my letter ready and went up to the lighthouse to mail it.

I read the plaque about savouring the sea and then I went in and got in line with the tourists. The lady was talking very quietly to the person at the head of the line. Everything was quiet in there and polite.

The lighthouse lady seemed to be the only person in Peggy's Cove who could keep the tourists quiet.

She had to weigh the letter because it was pretty thick and a bit heavy. She smiled at me and gave me all the stamps.

"Eddie told me all about your letter. It seems like it will be a very nice letter."

Some tourists were looking over my shoulder at the stamps going on.

"He's sending a big, long letter to his dad," she told them. "Isn't that nice?"

"Do you actually *live* in Peggy's Cove!" said the tourist.

"It would be a wonderful place to live," said another tourist, "it's so *realistic*!"

"I've got sadness, crime and danger in the letter," I said to the lighthouse lady.

"My, isn't that nice," she said, "isn't that nice!" And she gave me a funny look.

I was wondering whether I should mail the letter or

not. There were some things in there that weren't so true. Like about me being a crook, for instance. Mailing a letter is a funny thing. Once you drop it in the slot, you know you can't ever get it back. Even before it hits bottom, you know it's gone. It's not like saying something with your mouth that you're sorry for. You can always say, "I take it back. I'm sorry I said it." But a letter. You write it down and put it in the envelope and lick it and put the address and the stamps on. You're still alright. You can still tear it up and throw it away. But once you let a letter go in the slot, even before it hits bottom, you know you can *never* get it back.

I dropped the letter in the slot and heard the clunk as it hit bottom.

That same day, around supper-time, they caught the Drummer and me stealing.

15

It happened so fast!

Just as the Drummer picked up the bag a policeman and another man suddenly grabbed him by the arms.

Then the other man pointed at me and the owner of the restaurant came over and asked me to step outside with the policeman, the other man and the Drummer.

The Drummer was whistling like mad through his teeth. We walked down the rocks over near the lighthouse to get away from the crowd. Everybody was staring at us and some tourist's kids were pointing at the policeman holding the Drummer's arm. It was a beautiful evening. The sun was getting prepared for its dip into the sea and you could tell the tourists were getting a bit edgy. The gulls were just cruising and not saying "Don't" too much. There were a few sailboats on the sea. There was a bit of a breeze.

My mind was on jail mostly. Bars. Cement walls. An iron bed. A dirty piss pot in the corner. A sink with brown stains on it. I'm dressed in gray. There's a guy in the next cell. He's moaning and whimpering how sorry he is. Then the guard comes. I've got visitors. It's Mum and Dad and my sister Megan. Mum is crying because I'm so skinny and awful looking. Dad is staring at his feet muttering to himself how it's all his fault for going away like he did and I'm agreeing with him. I tell my sister she can have anything she wants out of my room because I won't be needing it anymore. She wants to know if she can have my binoculars too. They're not in my room, they're downstairs in the kitchen drawer — and I say sure, why not! Mum tells my sister not to be so heartless. Then they bring me my last meal. And my sister eats most of my chips.

The other man was the Drummer's parole officer. He had a kind face but he was sort of mad and he was asking the Drummer "Why?" and saying stuff like "How many times do you have to be told?"

Nobody was holding on to my arm or anything and I felt like running away and jumping off the rocks near the lighthouse over the cliff and into the sea.

The policeman brought his car from around the back of the restaurant. I remembered that on our trip out West I was in a police car for a while. But that was fun. That time I was a guest! This time I was a criminal! He put me and the Drummer in the back. After the door was closed the Drummer started whistling like mad and drumming his fingers on the back of the front seat. I couldn't believe he would start that at a time like this.

I hated the sound of it.

His whistling and drumming seemed to be getting louder and louder. The whistles were stabbing right into my brain. The policeman started the car. "We'll go to the other boy's place first," he was saying to the other man. "I'm told he lives just down at the bottom of the hill behind that shop there."

The whistling and drumming was louder than ever. I couldn't stand it anymore.

"Why don't you shut up!" I yelled. "Why don't you shut up, you stupid moron!"

The Drummer stopped and looked at me with hate in his face. His lip was curled up like a growling dog's. He looked like a different person. His face was a face I didn't even know.

I felt like smashing him.

I looked back at the lighthouse where I had mailed Dad's letter. I was hoping it would take off like a rocket and take the letter to outer space. Or maybe it would blow up and fall into the sea and sink forever.

"Alright, settle down back there," the policeman said. "We'll go down and talk to your father first. You live behind the shop don't you?"

Then I heard myself say a horrible thing. I didn't know I said it until after it came out.

"I haven't got a father," I said.

It was such a stupid thing to say. It was the Drummer who didn't have a father. Not me. What was I talking about?

"You mean your father's dead, or what?" said the policeman.

"No. I mean he's away. I mean I'm away. For the summer. I live with my aunt." I was totally confused.

"Well then you have a father then. Don't say you haven't got a father if you have a father. You're lucky to have a father. Lots of kids have no father. Kids these days. They say the dumbest things sometimes."

We pulled in Aunt Fay's laneway and got out of the car. The policeman went first. He went up to the door and knocked.

I never felt more stupid in my life, standing there, waiting for my own door to be opened!

The policeman introduced himself and we all went in.

"Your nephew here is in half a bit of trouble…"

While he was explaining the whole thing Aunt Fay

came over to me and put her arm over my shoulder. She reminded me so much of Dad just then that I looked at her hand on my shoulder a couple of times to make sure it was really hers.

They decided we'd all drive over to the Drummond's house.

"We'll make the final decisions what to do about all this over there," the policeman said. He was being very polite to Aunt Fay, calling her "Ma'am" and opening doors for her and helping her in the car.

We drove to the Drummer's and parked beside the big white pillars. The Drummer walked in first and opened the door so hard it banged against the wall.

His mother was smiling this crazy smile and inviting us into her big white room with the black piano as though we were going to have a party or something.

The parole officer was over talking to the Drummer and the mother and the policeman was with Aunt Fay and me at the other end of the room.

"We won't be pressing any charges because of the special circumstances in your case, because of the age of your nephew and because of your vouching for his conduct from now on. But I did want you both to witness first hand what this kind of thing can lead to." He sounded like he was reading out of a book.

Then Aunt Fay and I sat and listened to the policeman discussing with the parole officer and the mother what they were going to do with the Drummer. He was going to a "place" for a while.

When we left the house with the pillars the fog was down as thick as soup. As the policeman opened the car door Aunt Fay told him how much she appreciated his help and told him that we'd walk home if he didn't mind.

"It's a good mile, Ma'am, and it's a mite foggy."

"We'll make it," Aunt Fay said with her little laugh, "we'll make it."

We could hear a buoy out on the water moaning like it was in some terrible pain.

"I have a feeling your father's coming back," Aunt Fay said as we walked along the road in the fog.

"How do you know that?" I said.

"I know that because I know him. He's my brother you know, and I'm pretty sure he's just gone for a month or two to figure a few things out."

"What things?"

"Oh things I guess like being a father and being the provider for the family and being a husband and things like that that can get pretty scary sometimes."

"I was scared at the restaurant today."

"What did it feel like?"

"I felt like jumping over the cliff into the sea. I felt like running and running."

"Do you ever pretend you're talking to him when you're alone?"

I didn't say anything.

I wanted to ask her how she knew. The fog was moving around our feet as we walked along. Should I ask her? Usually I wouldn't ask a question like that. Usually I'd just keep those questions to myself.

"I heard you told the Drummer to shut up," she said after we walked along for a while.

"How did you know that?"

"Drummer's parole officer told me."

"I wanted to punch the Drummer's face."

"I'm glad."

"How did you know I sometimes talk to Dad when I'm alone?" I said.

"Because I've heard you. In your room."

I felt so embarrassed and stupid I stopped on the road and stared at my feet and started to sob like a baby.

I couldn't help it.

"That's alright. That's alright," Aunt Fay said. "Do you want to know something? Do you know everybody does that? Everybody in this world talks to people they love when they're not there? Everybody. Even people who don't have anybody. They make up people who love them and talk to them. Everybody does it."

I was leaning over, holding my stomach.

"Does Dad do it?"

"Definitely."

"Who does he talk to?"

"Right now, probably you."

Then it all came out. I told Aunt Fay all the stupid things I'd been doing. I told her everything that I put in the letter. I told her how phony the letter was. How I was really just trying to get him to come back. Trying to trick him.

After a while I started feeling quite a bit better.

You feel better when you let things out.

Aunt Fay told me Dad would probably realize what I was trying to do. When you love a person you always know why they do things.

"He's not stupid you know," Aunt Fay said.

It reminded me of what the Drummer once said to me.

I didn't feel like punching the Drummer anymore. I just felt sorry for him.

I wondered who he talked to when he was alone.

I wondered who he'd talk to when he was in "the place."

"There's one thing," I said to Aunt Fay before I

turned out my light in my room. "I'm never going fishing with Eddie and Wingding again. Never."

"Why? Oh, of course you are. What a thing to say. Of course you are. Here, I'll set your clock for you. What would your dad say if he heard you'd quit fishing. Why aren't you going fishing anymore?"

"Because I'm ashamed."

"Don't give it another thought. Now get a good night's sleep. You've had quite a day."

I turned out my light and turned towards the wall. Aunt Fay set my clock, said goodnight and closed the door.

After a few minutes when I was sure she had gone downstairs I spoke to the wall.

"I'm not, Dad. I'm just not. I'm too ashamed. What do Eddie and Wingding think of me now? Now that I'm a crook? I'm never fishing with them again. Never!"

Then I reached out and shut off the alarm on my clock.

16

When I woke up the next morning I couldn't believe what I saw.

Eddie and Wingding were sitting on the side of my bed!

It was seven o'clock.

"Aren't you fishing today?" Eddie said, and rubbed my head with his big rough hand.

Wingding smacked.

"We had a nice wait to hear about some storm warnings but it's alright. We're going out."

"We're going out?" I said, still trying to wake up.

"Sure. Water's nice and rough. Good for fishing!"

"You want me to go?"

"Smack."

"You want me to go?"

"Well now, if you have any more nice gin we can all

stay right here and have another garden party," Eddie said and looked at Wingding like he did when he was teasing him a bit. Wingding puckered his face all up and shook his head in a way that said no more gin, please, and smacked and looked like he was just forced to eat about ten lemons.

I felt like hugging him.

"You're some crook I hear. Can't even get arrested proper!" said Eddie and threw my pants and my shirt in my face. "Better stick to fishing, boy. Come on, get dressed, we're wasting good cod-time."

I was dressed in about a minute and heading out the door. Aunt Fay gave me a take-out sandwich and a big smile.

I was so happy I couldn't talk. I gave her a kiss and we took off.

So Eddie and Wingding didn't care what I had done with the Drummer.

And Dad wouldn't care either. I knew it now.

Everything was going to be alright.

So I thought.

There was no fog and no wind but the water in the cove was moving the boat up and down a lot more than usual and you could hear sloshing noises around the posts of the wharf.

Wingding wagged his head for a while and then we

put the fish boxes and the lines down in the boat and Eddie put on his orange gloves and we took off.

We stopped at our net and took our squid and mackerel bait and went out to our first stop. The sky was moving around and the lighthouse was disappearing in and out of the water. The boat was climbing up the water and sliding down the other side but there was no wind and no clouds and the sun was coming out of the sea like a red ball.

Wingding threw the anchor over and leaned away over to watch it go down.

Eddie cut up some squid and we baited our hooks.

Before we even got the hooks down far enough the cod came. Wingding's came up first. It was the biggest cod I ever saw. Wingding was grunting and smacking. He ripped it off the hook and threw it in the box without looking.

"Cod!" said Eddie and did his move.

Up came Eddie's cod. It was the same size.

"It's his brother!" Eddie said. "Can you sing? Can you sing? Sing 'Oh Canada!' for us, cod. Sing!"

My line jerked and I set the hook. I started pulling. Heavy. The boat slid down the other side of the water and I thought he got away. No. Heavy again.

"Cod!" I said.

When he came to the surface, I waited and looked,

then I lifted him very nicely into the boat. A perfect move!

The boat rolled and I fell backwards down in a fish box with the other two big cod and my cod on top of me.

Eddie and Wingding were pulling in two more. They ripped them off the hooks and threw them on top of me without looking.

Wingding was smacking and Eddie was saying, "Nice cod! Nice cod!"

I baited my hook again. I was laughing and talking to the squid as I cut his legs and his head off and he squirted up my wrist.

"Nice squid," I was saying, "nice squid."

The boxes were filling up and spilling over. We didn't care. We were throwing the big cod anywhere.

The lines were singing on the side of the boat. Eddie reached over with one hand in the middle of hauling and turned on his CB. I knew it was about nine o'clock. He always did that about nine o'clock. Nobody was talking over the channel. You could tell the other boats were busy too.

We pulled and hauled.

My arms were getting so tired that I couldn't set the hook right. My fish were coming up too slow. I lost one trying to take him out of the water.

Eddie and Wingding were hauling away. Fish after fish. I leaned back and closed my eyes. The boat was still climbing up and sliding down.

When I opened my eyes all I could see was a black blanket over the sun. The sky was blue straight up but over the sun was a huge black cloud.

And now there was a little wind. And some white water.

Then the cod stopped.

"They'll be back," Eddie said. "We can have a nice rest."

We listened to the voices now on the CB and cleaned up the boat a bit. We filled the boxes with the cod and pushed the rest over to one side so our lines wouldn't get tangled up.

Suddenly on the CB we got a call. Not a fancy call like you could get in the city in your car with a special number and fancy language and 10-4 and all that. When they'd call Eddie's boat to talk about the fishing or tell a joke to Eddie or something they'd just say, "Eddie, are you there?" And Eddie'd reach out and press his receiver button and say, "What did you want?"

And so we got the call.

"Eddie, are you there?"

"What did you want?"

117

"It's a message for the boy from his Aunt Fay from the shop."

"Oh yes?"

"You're to tell him that his dad will be coming in tomorrow sometime to pick him up."

"Oh isn't that nice. He wrote his dad a nice letter you know."

"He what?"

"Alright. Never mind. I'll tell him. His dad is coming in sometime tomorrow to get him. I'll tell him"

Just then the cod hit our lines again and Eddie said "Cod!" and we started hauling.

The news about Dad seemed to make all the strength come back into my arms.

"Your Dad is coming in sometime tomorrow to get you," Eddie said, ripping a big cod off his hook.

"Okay, Eddie, thanks for the message," I said, ripping a big cod off my hook.

"Smack! Smack!" said Wingding, ripping a huge cod off his hook.

Funny how when you're thinking of something else you can work fifty times as hard as if you're thinking about the work you have to do. Like shoveling the laneway. If you think about shoveling the laneway when you're shoveling the laneway your arms will get tired pretty fast. But if you think about something else, before you know it the laneway is shoveled and you hardly even notice it.

So we hauled cod and I thought about Dad. And we rested and joked and laughed and the wind got stronger and the boat got riding up farther and farther and shooting down the long slide and the water got blacker and whiter on the top of the waves and the sky got darker and the cod kept coming back and I thought about Dad.

I thought about going out fishing with him in a little rowboat on the Gatineau River when I was smaller and trolling along the shore and him rowing and making those little whirlpools with the oars that slide along past you when you're in the back seat. And when the rain came up and we got on a little beach and turned the boat over and got under it until the rain stopped. And how you could hear the rain tapping on the bottom of the boat right beside your ear.

The wind was pretty high now and the boat was rolling all over the place. We had so many fish in the bottom of the boat we were starting to get our lines tangled up. We were out of squid so we were cutting up the cod for bait. The sky was black and the wind was getting strong enough to bulge out our lines.

Eddie turned on the CBC to hear the time. It was nearly quitting time. You could tell by the program. Soon the two o'clock signal would come.

The white water was flying up over the boat. We were soaking wet.

Then we heard it.

"…at the sound of the long dash it will be two o'clock. Beep…Beep…Beep."

I pulled in my line. The cod had left. Wingding hauled his line and started wrapping it.

"…Beep…Beep…Beeeeeeeeeeep. Two o'clock Atlantic Standard Time."

"Shark!" yelled Eddie.

I saw him make his move but then he didn't start to haul. He was just holding onto the line as though it was stuck on the bottom.

"Shark!" Eddie said. "It'll take about a few minutes but he's not getting my gear!"

All of a sudden the rain fell down on top of us. I was half blinded but I could see Eddie starting to haul. One orange glove up a little bit then the next one grabbing on fast. It was like watching a dog holding on to a leather mitt letting go and grabbing a little more each time while you hold the other end.

"I want my gear," Eddie said. "You won't get my nice gear!"

A few more pulls. Wait. A long easy pull as the boat slid down the water then another long pull.

Wingding started the anchor winch so the shark wouldn't get tangled in the rope. If he got tangled he'd break the line and Eddie would lose his hook and his bar and a lot of good line.

Wingding watched the anchor come up with his face right against the crazy water. Then he lifted it into the boat, leaning away over, but Eddie was too busy to notice. Wingding got two gaffs from the front of the engine and gave me one.

He smacked and I knew what he meant.

We stood on both sides of Eddie and waited with our gaffs. When the shark came up we would help Eddie lift him from both sides.

The boat slid down a long, long slide sideways and Eddie hauled as though he had nothing on his hook.

We had no anchor now and the boat was doing crazy jumps. We went down one more slide and Eddie hauled quick.

Suddenly I saw the shark on the top of the water. He was very narrow just before his tail and blue on top and white on the bottom. And very wide at the head.

The boat tilted our way and he crashed against the side. Eddie started lifting him out of the water up the side of the boat. His line came out of the corner of the shark's mouth. Wingding reached over and slammed his gaff into the side of the shark's head and started to lift.

I slammed my gaff into the other side and started to lift.

Eddie pulled the line hard.

We lifted the shark until his head was a bit up over the edge of the boat. His head was very wide. The line was coming out of the corner of his mouth.

His eyes were wide open. One was looking at me. The other eye was looking at Wingding.

Eddie reached down for his knife with one hand while he held his line with his other. He was going to cut the shark's throat so it would open up its mouth and give Eddie back his gear.

I thought of the Widow Weed for a minute. "Never bring a shark on board," they said. I was glad we weren't going to. Eddie was going to cut its throat right there.

The wind was howling right through us and the rain was slashing our faces.

The shark was just hanging there, very still, staring at me and Wingding.

Then Eddie spoke to the shark.

"You won't be biting any nice holes in my nets any more now, will you?"

122

The knife was up, but all of a sudden the boat tilted the shark's way and gave him a lot of water. We were staring down into the black sea and the white foam and the shark went wild.

There was some quick thrashing and the next thing I knew Eddie was leaning away over with his hand right on the shark's snout and his face almost into the water. I saw Eddie's orange glove go down and I heard him scream. My gaff was in my hand with no weight on it. Wingding's flew up in the air. Eddie's hat went in the water and he stood up.

There was blood squirting out of his hand and where his thumb used to be there was ripped flesh and white bone.

He sat right down and his face was white. He grabbed his squirting hand with his other orange glove.

"Now isn't this nice!" he said as the wind howled. "Isn't this *nice!*"

I don't know what happened exactly after that.

I know Wingding started the boat and I got some rags for Eddie to hold on his hand. The blood was still squirting and Eddie was staring straight ahead.

As soon as Wingding started the motor and put the boat in gear he started looking over the side at the water. He was pointing at the water and smacking,

smacking, smacking. He was pointing and smacking at the water.

We circled around and headed for home and Wingding was still pointing in the water and he wouldn't stop smacking. When we pulled away from there, Wingding kept looking back and smacking and pointing. He was scaring me by the look on his face. His eyes were glistening and opening and shutting and he kept smacking in a vicious way.

He was acting like he wanted to kill somebody.

Eddie was staring straight ahead, sitting on our pile of cod, holding his hand. His snapped line was over the side of the boat whipping in the wind and the rain was slashing all around us.

Wingding had the motor full out and we crashed for home.

Suddenly I remembered the CB.

I got on and started calling.

I forgot all the "breaker breaker" stuff and just started yelling, "Anybody anybody, this is Eddie's boat, please answer, please answer…!"

Right away I got an answer.

"Okay, Eddie's boat. What's the matter? Where's Eddie?"

"Eddie's hurt. He needs a doctor. We're coming in!"

"What do you mean he's hurt?"

"Shark. Blood. Doctor!"

Then they clicked off.

The rain let up a bit and the wind got worse. Wingding was watching forward but every now and then he'd look back and point and smack like he was going to tear his mouth apart.

I could see the lighthouse and Wingding got us into the cove between the narrow rocks with the spray flying up on both sides.

Eddie just sat there with his one orange glove jamming the rags into his other bloody hand.

I never knew until then how really strong Wingding was. When we tied up to the wharf the tide was out and the boat was away down lower than usual.

Eddie was pretty weak. He stood up holding his hand out in front of himself with his other hand.

Wingding got behind Eddie and put his arm around his waist. Then he lifted him up like a store window dummy and climbed up the ladder with him. He was snapping at the rungs with his other hand like a hungry dog.

Some of the other fishermen helped Eddie off the wharf to a car. There was a doctor there with his bag.

I ran along behind. I could see the lighthouse lady in the back of the car. They helped Eddie in beside her.

The window on his side was half open. I looked in at Eddie.

"Nice that your dad's coming. Isn't that nice?" Eddie said. His face was white.

"Yes, that's nice. How do you feel?"

"Can you help Wingding clean the catch?"

"Yes. Do you feel alright?"

"It's a nice catch."

The car started moving away and I saw Eddie put his head on the lighthouse lady's shoulder.

The doctor was working on his hand.

Some tourists were taking pictures but not too many because the day was so black and the wind was blowing away their hats.

I looked back at the wharf and saw that Wingding was already back in the boat unloading the fish.

A box of fish when it's full is very heavy. There's a winch on the wharf the men use, if they're in when the tide is low, to hoist the boxes. Wingding wasn't using the winch. He was throwing the boxes from the boat right up onto the wharf. The boxes were landing on the wharf and the fish were sliding all over the place.

I got the big shovel and started shoveling them back in the boxes while Wingding threw them up. The wind was getting wilder. All you could see was fish flying up onto the wharf and landing and bouncing and sliding around.

Then Wingding's face came up the ladder. I can remember exactly how it looked. I have the picture right here in my mind.

His snout was more blunt than ever and his wrinkles were all pulled back towards his ears as if something was stretching his face from behind. His nostrils were collapsing and blowing and his mouth was glued shut.

And his eyes, away in there, were glistening, burning.

Then his hand came up to the top rung. He had his knife out.

He looked like he was ready to kill somebody!

There was a small group of tourists standing near the cutting table waiting for Wingding to start. There was another group on the road, standing close together, because of the wind, waiting.

I loaded the cutting table with the shovel and Wingding stepped up with his knife.

He was using four strokes. One for the belly, one for the head, two for the back fins and rip; he threw the first two that he cleaned, the heads, the guts and the back-fin, as hard as he could at the group of tourists on the wharf. They put their hands up to protect themselves and started to back up. Then they turned around and started to hurry off the wharf.

One tourist got a fish head and a string of guts right square in the back of his tourist coat. One tourist turned around to get a quick picture of Wingding throwing guts and heads. He wasn't quick enough. Just as he snapped his picture, his camera, his hands and his face got splattered with the insides and head of a big, fat cod.

Now everything was going straight up in the air and taking off in the wind. Wingding and the wind were both going crazy. The wind was blowing everything onto the side of the fish-house and the gulls were crashing into the wall and fighting for their dinner all the way down to the water.

Then the wind changed and all the fish waste came showering down on the tourists on the road like a rain of garbage. They were screaming and running and picking things off their hats and their shoulders and their kids.

And Wingding's arms were moving up and down and the clean cod were dropping into the tub, one every eight seconds — plop — into the tub — plop — another — eight seconds — into the tub, and up flying in the air were the heads that all looked like my dad's friend Frank with the eyes bulging and the pointy teeth — and the fish stomachs and hearts and air sacs and livers and blood and slime and fins all flying in the crazy wind and the tourists running and Wingding smacking and his eyes glistening and burning and his face looking like he wanted to kill somebody.

We salted down the cod in the fish-house and put them in the barrel. Then Wingding went and lay down on some sacks in the corner with his face to the wall in the fish-house.

I stood there for a long time hoping he would turn around and smack at me and then maybe we could talk for a while.

But he didn't turn around.

"Do you want to come over to Aunt Fay's and see if she has any gin?"

"Smack," to the wall.

"Eddie will be alright. The doctors will fix his hand."

Silence.

"Tomorrow's Sunday. No fishing tomorrow. Maybe we can go into Halifax and see him in the hospital."

"Smack."

I waited for another long time until I thought he was asleep. Then I went quietly out the fish-house door onto the wharf. I closed the door quietly, holding it so the wind wouldn't slam it and wake him up.

129

Suddenly he was smacking like crazy. I went back in because I thought he was calling me but he wasn't. His face was still to the wall. I could tell by the smacks he was talking to himself.

Or was he?

I didn't think of it then but now I know he was talking to somebody he loved. He was talking to Eddie.

Alone, pretending Eddie was there. Talking to him. Telling him what he was going to do.

I didn't think of it then.

I guess I couldn't have. Even if I had thought of it, I wouldn't have understood what he was saying.

Wingding loved Eddie. And he was going to do something to prove it. He was telling him about it right now.

Something like I had been doing with Dad.

17

That night the storm got worse.

Aunt Fay and I had supper and she closed the gift shop early because the wind and rain blew all of the tourists away. The wind was slashing the rain on the windows and the old house was creaking like an ancient ship in a stormy sea.

Dad was coming the next evening.

I asked Aunt Fay if we could drive into Halifax the next day to see Eddie in the hospital and if we could take Wingding. She said she'd have to drive in to pick up Dad anyway, so we could go a little early and see Eddie before we went to the airport.

That made me feel good.

I got my pajamas on, then Aunt Fay came up and sat on the edge of my bed. I was lying there trying to read a book but I couldn't concentrate on it.

"You were right," I said, "he is coming back."

"He's a good man, your father."

"So's Eddie. So's Wingding."

"So are *you*, young man."

"What do you mean?"

"Wingding couldn't have called on the CB. Your warning got the car and doctor ready. If it hadn't been for you things might have been very serious. It's a long wait for a doctor here. And the closest hospital is in Halifax. A long way with a serious injury like Eddie had. All the fishermen are talking about what a hero you are."

I was looking right up into Aunt Fay's nice face.

"I wish Dad was here right now," I said.

We talked a little more and then I must have dozed off because I suddenly realized my light was out.

The wind was rattling the window.

Aunt Fay was still sitting on the bed.

"Can you look out and see if Wingding's light is on in the schoolhouse?" I whispered to her.

She said it was and gave me a kiss on the forehead and left, closing the door behind her.

I crawled deeper into my bed and went to sleep. But I woke up many times. Or maybe it was just in my dreams that I woke up. I thought I could see the waves crawling half-way up the lighthouse then crashing back and shaking the whole point. I thought I could see the shark munching on Eddie's thumb like a kind of pretzel, smacking his jaws and rolling his eyes, one towards me, one towards Wingding. And Wingding smacking right back at him and the two of them staring at each other. I thought I could see Aunt Fay with her hands cupped beside her eyes, peering in the schoolhouse window and catching the Drummer with stacks of Indian leather belts and Canadian coats and soapstone carvings and plastic shopping bags full of loot piled up in there. And I thought I saw a boy who looked just like me being chased by mobs of tourists, all of them yelling and angry and pointing at me and waving binoculars and cameras and gunning the motors of their Winnebagos to run me down. And I thought I heard the gulls cry and the wind howl. And I thought I heard a motor starting up, a bubbly, frothy sound, the sound of Eddie's boat.

I slept until about ten o'clock. The sun was shining in my window and the wind was still howling a bit but I could tell it was going to be a nice day for Dad's arrival.

Downstairs Aunt Fay was on the phone.

"No, he's not," she was saying. "I checked his place. He's not there. His light is on. It looks like he left early this morning."

"Wingding?" I said.

"Yes," Aunt Fay said as she hung up. "Somebody

took Eddie's boat out this morning. It must have been Wingding. One of the boys is going out to see if he's alright. They say it was a very terrible sea out there last night and this morning."

I ran down to the wharf. Some of the fishermen were sitting in their boats testing their radios.

By twelve o'clock there were three boats out looking.

No sign of Eddie's boat.

By three o'clock they called the shore patrol and described the boat.

At four they got the call back.

It was Eddie's boat alright!

And the man on board, how is he?

Nobody?

Nope. Just a shark with his throat cut!

By the time Aunt Fay left for Halifax to pick up Dad there was a huge crowd around the wharf waiting for Eddie's boat to be driven back.

I waited, my feet dangling over the edge of the wharf. Then I heard the motor and saw the boat turning in through the narrows. She had her anchor up, dangling from the winch, jammed there.

I had to see for myself that Wingding wasn't there. Funny, I thought that if I looked in the boat I'd be able to see him there even if nobody else could.

But I knew in my heart that he wasn't.

All I could see were the empty fish boxes, the gaffs, the lines wrapped neatly.

And the red and white gash in an ugly throat.

The guy driving said he left everything as he found it so we could see for ourselves.

Everybody was talking at once to everybody else.

"Brought the shark on board, cut its throat, then fell over lifting the anchor."

"He always leaned out to watch the anchor come up."

"How in the name of God did he ever get that fish on board all alone?"

"Look, there's two fishing lines in the shark — one of them's cut."

"The cut one is Eddie's," I said. "Tell them to open him up. There's an orange glove in there."

"Must have leaned over too far — high wind — boat off balance — boat running pretty good with the wind — just left him there — wouldn't have a chance in that water."

"Leave it to Wingding."

"Well, he got Eddie's glove back!"

"That he did. Good shape too."

"Any sign of the thumb?"

"Pretty hard to find a thumb in that mess. Mostly digested anyway."

"Wingding's a hero!"

Wingding's gone.

Forever.

Poor Wingding!

18

Aunt Fay pulled her car into the laneway beside the shop. I could see Dad getting out. Aunt Fay was pointing to the wharf and he was looking over.

I ran off the wharf down the road and across to the shop.

I wasn't crying.

I banged into him trying to put my arms around him. He kind of lifted me up. He felt good.

We were standing in the perfect spot to take the perfect picture. The tourists were all around us. The gulls were going crazy. It was a perfect day in Peggy's Cove.

Dad started talking.

"I heard that Wingding drowned. That's sad. I know he was a friend of yours. I'm sorry."

"I really liked him," I said.

"I wish I'd met him."

"He couldn't talk. I keep imagining his face in the water as the boat floated away. Trying to say something. Poor Wingding. Going 'smack' in the water as the boat floated away."

The tourists were all arguing and taking pictures of each other. One guy, trying to get a close-up of a seagull, fell head first into the cove water and stood up draped with parts of fish skins and slime.

The gulls were crabbing and crying.

But Dad and I were standing in a circle of silence all our own.

"Are you coming home?"

"Yes, I went a little nuts for awhile but I'm okay now."

"Is it true you talk to yourself?" I said, looking right in his eyes.

"Sure it's true. Who told you that?"

"Aunt Fay," I said.

"Well, she should know," Dad laughed. "She talks to herself too. Don't you? Doesn't everybody?"

A gull was posing for a picture on the nose of Eddie's boat.

"I guess so," I said. Dad had his arm around my shoulders.

"How are you, anyway? I hear you're a bit of a hero," he said.

"Sort of."

I paused.

"I wrote you a letter, you know. Mailed it two days ago. I guess you'll never get it."

"Probably not. I won't be going back to where I was. You can tell me what's in it anyway." We started to walk towards Aunt Fay's house.

We stopped.

We were standing in the same spot that I had stood on with the policeman and the Drummer.

"I talk to myself too, you know," I said.

"Oh? And who do you talk to? Who do you pretend is there?" Dad said.

I looked at him like I never looked at him before.

"You," I said.

"That's funny," Dad said, "lately most of my conversations have been with you. That's pretty nice isn't it?"

"Yes," I said. "That's pretty nice."

Then I knew by his face that everything was going to be alright.

I put one foot over the other and sort of leaned on him like in a picture of us at home on our wall. The picture has Dad and me. Dad is standing up straight with his hands deep in his pockets and his legs apart. He has on an old railway cap we saved from a trip we once took out West. In the picture, I'm standing beside him with my hands in my pockets and I'm leaning on him a bit. I have on my railroad hat too. My left foot is crossed over my right one and I'm sort of propped up against him. In the picture, if he moved I would probably fall over.

In the picture, my ear comes up to his belt.

Now, my ear came up to about his chest. I was leaning on him just a bit.

A camera in my head started working. I could see us there, surrounded by millions of tourists and gulls.

I imagined the camera moving back, back and up, until you could see the whole of Peggy's Cove with the foam smashing away at the lighthouse and the pretty colors and the boats out at sea and the tiny tourists running around and the little white dots that were gulls.

And the tiny still figures in the middle of it all. That was Dad and me.